Queen of Poison

Lily Bloom Cozy Mystery Series

by Lyndsey Cole

CONTENTS

CHAPTER 1

Chapter 1

Lily's phone was ringing nonstop. *I don't have time for this right now.* "Hello Mom. What's the problem?"

Iris blurted out in her usual dramatic fashion, "Someone stole your father."

That got Lily's attention. "What?" This was more intense than Iris usually managed.

"Your father is gone."

"Of course he's gone. Dad died three years ago. Did you just notice this today?" Lily wondered if Iris had overdone it with her medical marijuana again.

"Don't be a smart aleck. Someone stole the urn with his ashes."

Lily picked up her quilted tote covered with a colorful arrangement of flowers and her appointment book. "Meet me at Beautiful Blooms. I'll be there in ten minutes." She hung up before Iris had a chance to say any more nonsense. Lily still missed her father. He had been the mediator between the three Bloom women—Lily, her sister Daisy, and their mom, Iris. He was easy going and had a great sense of humor which always squashed the tension if the women got too testy. Lily had her father to thank for her Beautiful Blooms Flower Shop too. She'd used the money he left her to buy the building and get it started, against her mother's wishes. Iris considered it a boring choice but it had been Lily's dream and the town was wildly supportive of her business.

"Come on Rosie. You can come to work with me today." Rosie wagged her tail and rushed to the door. Lily let them out the back door and walked to her minivan, still thinking about her dad. She was shocked when she looked up and saw a red mustang convertible driving into her neighbor's driveway. *I wonder who is visiting Ryan Steele this early in the day.* A tall red headed woman got out of the car and grabbed a suitcase from the back seat.

Lily realized she had stopped and was gawking at the newcomer. The red head looked up and waved to Lily. "Good morning."

Lily returned the wave and quickly got into her car. Ryan hadn't mentioned anyone coming to visit. Ever since he'd been hired as the permanent police chief of Misty Valley she didn't see much of him. But still, she thought this would have been newsworthy. He never even mentioned that he had a girlfriend which was odd since she thought he was interested in her. *I knew there had to be a catch. Everyone thought he was perfect,* she thought.

Iris's yellow, convertible VW bug was already parked in front of Lily's flower shop. *This day is not starting well.* "Come on Rosie. Let's get this over with." They walked through the front gate and small garden in front of the shop, opening the door to the familiar jingle from her antique bell.

Iris was having an animated conversation with Daisy about the disappearance of the urn. "I never told you girls, but that urn is very valuable. It was handed down from my grandmother to my mother to me. I bet whoever stole it is in for a surprise when they discover it's filled with someone's ashes." Iris laughed at that thought. They turned their attention to Lily when she walked in. "Lily. What should we do about it? Call your handsome cop friend?"

"Call him if you want to. He has a tall red head visiting so he might be busy," Lily said with disdain as she threw her tote and appointment book onto her cluttered desk in the back work room.

Daisy laughed. "What's the matter Lily? I thought you didn't like the handsome Ryan Steele. It sounds like you're a little jealous."

The brass bell above the door jingled again as Tamara Biotchi made her grand entrance. "You won't believe it. Someone broke into my house and stole my grandmother's antique table."

Lily, Iris and Daisy all stopped what they were doing and looked at Tamara. "Stole your table?"

"It was a small table, but very valuable. Who would do a thing like that?"

Iris sounded furious. "Someone stole my husband. What's going on in this town?"

Tamara looked at Iris, full of concern. "Your husband is dead. Are you sure he was stolen?"

The door jingled as Ryan Steele and his beautiful lady friend walked in.

"The urn with his ashes were stolen, you ninny. The urn is valuable. And of course the ashes are priceless to me," she remembered to add.

Ryan looked concerned. "What was stolen?"

Tamara and Iris both started talking about the stolen table and husband, their voices escalating so nothing could be understood.

Ryan held up his hands. "One at a time. Did I hear you say your husband?" Ryan finally got the story straight. "Come to the station and fill out a report. You two aren't the only ones in town to have had something stolen." He turned his attention back to the striking person standing quietly by his side. "This is Jennifer. She's staying with me for a few days. I just wanted to show her around town before I get busy at work."

Lily stormed to the back room without any greeting. Ryan watched her leave and asked Daisy, "What's wrong with your sister this morning? Did she get up on the wrong side of the bed?"

Daisy smirked. "You'll have to ask her, I guess."

"No time now. Come on Jennifer. I'll walk you to the library, then you'll be on your own till lunch." Ryan looked once more toward the back and shook his head mumbling, "I can't figure her out."

Tamara and Iris left for the police station, still discussing the stolen items.

Daisy found Lily standing at the design table, stabbing yellow chrysanthemums into foam for a big funeral piece. "What's your problem Lily? A tad jealous?" She loved needling her big sister about the on-again-off-again attraction Lily had with the handsome, and everyone had thought eligible, Ryan Steele.

Lily kept working furiously. "So he has a gorgeous girlfriend. Big deal. I have other things to think about now."

Daisy laughed. "If you say so."

Lily finally slowed down and looked at Daisy. "Why does he get under my skin so easily?"

"Duh. Because you like him."

"Not today." Lily finished the arrangement and put it in the cooler. "Now I have to get going on the arrangement for the Art in Bloom opening at the museum tonight."

Daisy wrapped a bouquet of roses and baby's breath. "Pretty sweet that you got to do the centerpiece of the show. Who's sitting with us at the reception tonight?"

Lily scowled. "Ryan was supposed to but I don't want him bringing that woman. You, Mom, Tamara, Marigold and Melinda."

"There's room for Jennifer too. You may as well find out who your competition is."

Lily looked at Rosie. "Do you want to come and take that seat?"

Rosie wagged her tail, always up for an outing.

Daisy laughed. "She is a celebrity ever since she caught that murderer and saved your life. Maybe you could sneak her in."

***

The Misty Valley Museum was in an historical building owned by Marion Barry, an eccentric lady with a passion for floral artwork. The brick and clapboard museum was surrounded by a lovely perennial garden on Lupine Lane, just down the street from Lily's Beautiful Blooms Flower Shop.

Lily had her arrangement all set and ready to deliver by mid-afternoon. It had tall royal blue delphinium, green bells of Ireland and orange lilies nested in moss flowing over the sides of a dark blue handmade ceramic dish. She had an antique mirror to place it on, giving the effect of an island garden on a pond. "What do you think Daisy?"

Daisy's hand went over her heart. "It's stunning Lily. Those colors and the reflection are absolutely beautiful. Do you need help moving it to the museum?"

Lily looked around the shop. "It's pretty quiet. Let's lock the front door so you can come too. We can get a quick preview of the other arrangements while we're there."

Lily carefully placed the arrangement in her van and they drove the half mile to the museum.

Elizabeth Stevens, the museum director, was greeting everyone as they delivered the various flower displays for the Art in Bloom opening. It was an annual event where anyone could pick a painting and interpret it with flowers. The museum had been sponsoring the event for several years and it was very popular.

She fluttered her hands when she saw Lily. "I knew you would make a magnificent arrangement. Follow me. I have a table all set up for you right inside the entryway." Elizabeth's high heels clattered on the slate tiles. "Everyone will see your flowers as soon as they walk in. Marion insisted that her favorite floral painting would be the centerpiece this year. Put it here. Right next to the painting."

Lily carefully put the mirror and flowers on the small table next to the painting. They all stood back. Elizabeth gasped. "I hope Ms. Barry isn't upset if her painting gets upstaged by your flowers. I've never seen a more striking arrangement."

Lily blushed slightly from all the compliments. "Thank you, Elizabeth. Do you mind if Daisy and I take a quick peek at the other arrangements?"

Elizabeth patted Lily's shoulder. "Go right ahead. This is my favorite time of year. The Art in Bloom show brings so many more people into our special museum than any other art show we have. You will be back tonight for the reception I hope."

Lily nodded. "Of course. I have a table full of friends and family."

Elizabeth clapped her hands together. "That's great. Ms. Barry is speaking tonight at the dinner. She hasn't always felt well enough to attend for the last few years. She's excited about her new painting and since her niece and nephew are coming, she didn't want to miss this year. I'll be sure to introduce you."

Lily and Daisy started to walk away but Elizabeth stopped them, looking concerned. "Have you heard about the recent antique thefts happening around town?"

Lily was surprised word had spread so fast. "What have you heard?"

"Tamara Biotchi had an antique table stolen and several other people had antiques taken from their homes." She lowered her voice to a whisper. "I have extra security here at the museum. I don't think many people know just how valuable these paintings are."

Lily looked around. "I'm sure you are very busy. We'll take a quick look around and see you tonight at the reception."

"Thank you, Lily. Your arrangement is perfect. See you tonight." Elizabeth turned her attention to another person coming with an arrangement, oohing and aahing over their flowers.

Lily and Daisy giggled as they made their way up the grand staircase to the upstairs galleries. "She's wound tighter than an antique clock. Hope she doesn't have high blood pressure. This extra stress won't do her any good."

Daisy stopped at the top of the stairs in front of a portrait of Marion Barry. "She looks like a dour old lady. This flower arrangement of dark blue monkshood with a white calla and one red rose does capture the mood of the painting quite well. Don't you think?"

"And the black cloth over the table with a pair of old metal frame glasses creates a somber image for sure. It will be interesting to meet her. She never married and has always been a bit of a recluse. I wonder who will inherit all her wealth."

Daisy and Lily stood shoulder to shoulder looking at the painting and flowers. "I hope the monkshood isn't some type of foreboding that a deadly foe is near." Lily shook that thought away and headed back down the stairs. "Let's get back to the shop and clean up so we have time to get ready for the opening tonight."

Chapter 2

Daisy was overloaded with an armful of fancy dresses as she walked into Lily's house. They had a tradition of helping each other decide on what looked best. Daisy loved to get dressed up but Lily preferred to dress casually most of the time. Typically, it was Daisy helping her older sister. It had been like this their whole life.

They pranced around in their underwear, holding up dresses and looking in the full length mirror. Lily grabbed an emerald green slinky, silky dress with a floral design going from one shoulder to the waist. Daisy tried to steal it back. "That's my favorite dress."

Lily swung it away from Daisy's fingers. "Ha. I got it first. I want to look extra special tonight."

Daisy pulled a red flowery silk dress from the pile. "Why is that?"

"Just because." Lily slipped the green fabric over her head. It shimmered down her lean body. She twirled and felt the sensuous fabric tickle her thighs. "What do you think?"

Daisy paused to look intently at Lily. "I think you want to look nice for Ryan Steele. Get him away from that red head." Laughing, she added, "Maybe you shouldn't have been so standoffish in the past. He got sick of waiting for you to make up your mind."

Lily angrily denied that accusation. "I don't care about Mr. Steele. I want to look nice since my arrangement is the centerpiece of the show. I need to look my best in case Nina Baldwin is there to take photos and write an article."

"If you say so," Daisy said mockingly.

A knock on the back door startled Lily. "I wonder who that is. Mom is picking us up but she wouldn't bother to knock." Lily went to the door feeling festive and happy.

Ryan Steele was standing outside looking drop dead good-looking, waiting as if she was supposed to be expecting him. Lily was speechless.

He slowly scanned her from naked toes to blond ponytail and whistled his approval. "Wow. You look incredible." He grinned. "You might want to put some shoes on though. I told you I would give you a ride. Don't you remember?"

Lily fidgeted and blushed. "Oh. I made other plans since you have a friend visiting."

"Jennifer?" Ryan chuckled. "My sister? Is that why you've been avoiding me?"

Lily felt her face get hotter and hotter. She stuttered and stammered, feeling like a complete fool, which was how Ryan Steele usually made her feel. "Iris is picking us up. I'll meet you there?" was all she could manage to say in a somewhat strangled voice.

Ryan leaned close to Lily's ear. "You look absolutely beautiful. You should dress up more often." He straightened back up and winked. "See you there. Oh, and by the way, try not to get your dress caught in the door when you slam it. I'd hate for someone else to have to rescue you."

Lily watched him walk to his car. He was never going to let her forget their first encounter when she so clumsily slammed her car door catching her skirt and making her trip and fall. His scent lingered and she silently gave herself a good kick for jumping to the wrong conclusion about Jennifer.

Daisy tapped her arm. "What just happened? Was that Ryan?"

Iris drove in honking which saved Lily from having to make an explanation to Daisy. They piled into the back of her VW bug and headed to the museum. Marigold Harris was in the passenger seat, happily looking around as though she could actually see what was out the window. Being blind didn't slow her down at all.

It was a short half mile drive to the Misty Valley Museum. The street was lined with cars and people were making their way into the main entrance. Iris swerved her bug into a parking spot between two big SUVs, almost taking off her front fender. "How's that for maneuvering?"

Marigold responded with two thumbs up. "I didn't hear any metal crunching so it's fine by me."

Iris helped Marigold out of the car, holding her left arm and giving a running commentary about what was happening. Marigold had her white cane in her right hand tapping along the sidewalk. Daisy and Lily walked behind.

"Wait up you guys." Lily turned around to see Melinda Biotchi and Jack Weaver hurrying to catch up. "Can we sit with you?"

"Of course." Lily asked Jack, "How is it going at the greenhouse?"

Jack looked content. "I couldn't be happier. It's much better than working at the Misty Valley Country Club." He looked at Melinda. "I think Tamara is even starting to like me."

Lily laughed. "Wonders will never cease."

They entered the museum and were greeted by Elizabeth Stevens who was standing next to Lily's arrangement and the floral painting. "Hello. Hello." She leaned toward Lily and whispered, "Everyone loves your flowers. How daring to put blue and orange together, and the mirror makes the flowers and the painting sparkle from the lighting. Ms. Barry is extremely pleased with how the whole show is looking. She's looking forward to meeting you."

Lily beamed. "Thank you. I'm curious to meet her, too."

"I'll find you when she has a moment. Oh, and Nina Baldwin will be taking photos. Be sure to have her get one of you next to your flowers."

Lily glanced at Daisy to see if she heard that exchange. Daisy nodded slightly. Iris and Marigold were already ahead so Daisy pulled Lily away from Elizabeth and they hurried to catch up.

Iris was describing the paintings to Marigold and letting Marigold guess what flowers were used in the arrangement based on the scent. She did an excellent job figuring it all out and seemed to enjoy it more than Iris even though she couldn't see anything. Lily smiled as she watched the two older women. Iris was so content ever since Marigold moved in with her. It gave Iris a focus away from her two daughters, which was good for all of them. And Marigold was thrilled to be out of the nursing home.

The museum was stunning with all the flowers. A trio of violin, cello and piano played classical music at the side of the main staircase. The mixture of flowers perfumed the rooms. All in all, it was perfect.

Lily felt a gentle touch on her arm. Elizabeth was pulling her away from her family and pointing toward an elderly woman standing off to the side. She whispered, "Ms. Barry is free and wants to meet you now."

Lily was surprised to see how tall and straight Marion Barry was. She looked elegant in her black dress with a dark red shawl draped around her shoulders. Her silvery gray hair was cut stylishly just below her chin. She smiled warmly as Elizabeth escorted Lily over and introduced them. She was much warmer in person than how the artist captured her in her portrait.

Ms. Barry extended her hand to Lily. "I'm so glad to meet you Ms. Bloom. I've heard a lot about you from Elizabeth and she was absolutely right when she said you would put together an arrangement to complement my newest painting. And it's wonderful that Misty Valley finally has a flower shop. If you ever need anything, let me know."

Lily was having trouble finding a reply to this generous offer. Suddenly the lights went out. Several seconds of silence were broken by screaming and scuffling. Lily felt a weight fall against her chest. She held on, confused about what was happening. Crashing sounded from the main entryway.

What felt like forever actually only lasted for a few minutes before the lights were back on. Lily saw that she was holding Marion Barry. Iris and Daisy appeared at her side. They both looked wild eyed. "What just happened?"

Lily gently lowered Marion onto an antique Queen Anne chair nearby. "I have no idea but we need to get help for Ms. Barry. Call 911. Is Ryan here yet?" She looked around frantically but couldn't see him through all the chaos.

Elizabeth hovered, wringing her hands and sobbing. "Oh dear. Oh dear. Is she alright?"

Lily looked at Elizabeth and shook her head as she felt for a pulse on Marion Barry's wrist. She felt like she was going to faint. "I think she's dead."

Chapter 3

A portly middle aged woman pushed Lily aside. "What have you done to Marion?" If looks could kill, the look that hit Lily would have dropped her in an instant.

"What have *I* done? She fell into me when the lights went out. All I did was catch her. Who are you?"

The woman stretched to her full height which was at least two inches below Lily's chin. "I am Ruth Walsh, Ms. Barry's personal secretary. I've been at her side for the last thirty years." She looked Lily up and down before asking with contempt, "And who are *you?*"

Lily realized there was a lot of emotion running through everyone at the moment and decided not to take Ruth Walsh's comments personally. "I'm sorry for your loss. Elizabeth had just introduced me to Ms. Barry. I'm Lily Bloom. I did the arrangement to go with her new floral painting."

Ruth's nose wrinkled in distaste. "Oh. You did that ghastly arrangement? And you call yourself a florist?"

Ryan Steele showed up at Lily's side. "Your mother said you need help."

"In more ways than one at the moment." She managed to ignore Ruth and nod her head toward Ms. Barry slumped in the chair. Her face was already a pasty gray. "She fell into me when the lights went out. I think she may have had a heart attack or something."

The EMTs entered with a stretcher. "Clear the way please. We need to get through." They placed Marion's body on the stretcher and rushed her into the ambulance.

Ruth turned her attention back to Lily. "You'll pay for this young lady. This is all your fault." She turned and left, presumably to follow the ambulance to the hospital.

Ryan watched that interaction. "Why does she think it's your fault?"

Trying to remain calm, Lily took a deep breath. "I think she's just upset about losing a dear friend. At least I hope that's the reason."

Lily was stunned by the events of the last fifteen minutes. She looked up and was blinded by the flash of a camera going off in her face. It took her eyes a few seconds to adjust and see Nina Baldwin snapping away. This was going to be a much more interesting story than covering a relatively boring Art in Bloom opening night.

Nina grabbed Lily's arm. "Come over here," she said excitedly. "I want to get a photo of you with your flowers and the new painting." Lily stumbled along with her even though she knew she did not want to be in the photo. Nina got her shot, then was dashing off to photograph more drama.

Daisy found Lily. "This is turning into a circus. I overheard Marion Barry's niece and nephew talking about her death. They expect to be millionaires now. It didn't sound like they were disappointed about the turn of events. Do you think they might have murdered her for the money?"

Lily shushed Daisy. "Don't even talk like that. No one is saying it's murder. She just fell over. Onto me. How could that be murder?"

Daisy toned her voice down to a mere whisper. "That's what I'm hearing. People think she was murdered for the inheritance."

Lily pulled Daisy off to the side. "That just makes a more interesting story than saying she died of natural causes. We'll find out soon enough. Here comes Ryan. Maybe he knows more."

Ryan put his hand on Lily's back. She felt his warmth through the thin fabric of her dress. The warmth spread right to her fingertips. "Everything okay?"

Lily couldn't stop the question from blurting from her mouth. "Was she murdered?"

"I don't know but I have to close the museum. Elizabeth Stevens is going to make an announcement soon asking everyone to leave. Could you check on Jennifer? I won't be home for a while."

Lily's gaze swept the room. "I'll be happy to get away from all this." She looked sympathetically at Ryan. "We'll get some food and invite Jennifer to my house. Don't worry about her."

Elizabeth stood half way up the stairs with her husband, Kirk Stevens, at her side. "Everyone. Please quiet down. I have to make an announcement. As you may have heard already, the museum's founder, Marion Barry has been taken to the hospital. After discussing the matter with the museum board of directors, we have decided to cancel the opening for tonight and reschedule for tomorrow night. Marion won't be able to be with us but we are confident that this is what she would have wanted. So, please accept my sincere apology about this unexpected turn of events and come back tomorrow to help us launch Art in Bloom properly. Thank you. The museum will be closed in ten minutes."

Daisy looked puzzled. "Is she still alive?"

"I don't think so. Maybe they just don't want to say anything until all the facts are determined. Let's find Iris and Marigold, get something to eat and go to my house."

***

"Mom, swing by the Misty Valley Market. I'll run in and buy a couple of Billy's premade pizzas. They're all ready to pop in the oven." Lily reached for her purse, feeling around on the floor. "I can't find my purse. Daisy, give me some money, I'll pay you back."

It took longer than expected to get to the market since everyone was pulling out of the museum at the same time. And it seemed like many others had the same idea about buying a quick dinner at the market. This would be great for Billy. He had complained to Lily that the opening was going to cut into his normal evening sales.

Lily managed to get inside before too many other hungry people and grabbed the last two pizzas. Lily saw Marion Barry's niece and nephew arguing by the deli counter. Lily watched them while she waited in line to pay. Maggie was laughing and giggling but Jared was unsmiling and kept telling Maggie to shut up and quit leaning on him. Lily couldn't help but wonder what their life was like and how it would change with the death of their aunt. From what Daisy heard, they expected to inherit a lot of money but maybe Marion was leaving it all to the museum and her favorite charities. Lily laughed at that thought and how it would upset those two greedy relatives.

She paid and got back into the car. "Okay. Next stop, my house."

The chatter in the car was getting pretty loud with Iris, Daisy and Marigold trying to talk over each other with different versions of what happened and what might still happen. Iris managed to get to Lily's house. Daisy carried the pizzas inside and turned on the oven while Lily went next door to check on Jennifer.

Lily explained to Jennifer, "There was a situation and Ryan has to work late."

"A situation?"

Lily clarified. "Actually, the founder died and the director closed the museum so the police could try to sort out what happened." Lily changed the subject, she didn't want to get into any speculation about the death. "We have pizza in the oven. Care to join us?"

"That sounds great. I've got a couple of bottles of wine. Should I bring that?"

"Definitely." Lily held the door open. "You're okay with a dog I hope."

Jennifer laughed. "Ryan told me all about your amazing Rosie. I can't wait to meet her."

Lily thought Jennifer might be okay. She liked dogs and she *wasn't* Ryan's girlfriend. Maybe this day could end on a decent note after all.

The pizza cooked and made the house smell delicious. Talk turned to how hungry they were as they sat in the living room sipping the wine.

Iris eyed Jennifer. "Your brother is somewhat of a mystery to all of us here. Got any good stories to share?"

Jennifer had a sly grin. "He warned me about you, Iris. Sure, I don't mind giving a little information. Just don't tell him it came from me."

Iris was like a prosecutor, cross examining a witness in a trial. "How old is he?"

"Thirty-two."

"Ever been married?"

"No." Jennifer hesitated before adding, "But he was engaged."

Iris jumped all over that news. "What happened?"

"I'm not sure you should here this from me."

"Yes. Yes." The others all chimed in together, leaning forward excitedly.

"Well, okay. His fiancé, Carla, broke it off."

"Why?"

"She ran off with his best friend. Ryan was heartbroken and hasn't dated since." Jennifer glanced at Lily. "He's been happy since he got hired to be the police chief here in Misty Valley. I think he needed to move away and start over."

The timer on the oven interrupted the conversation and saved Jennifer from anymore grilling from Iris. Lily went into the kitchen to get the pizza. "I'll bring it out. We can eat around the coffee table."

Jennifer followed Lily. "Can I help? Tell me where the plates are and I'll bring them out."

Lily took the pizza out of the oven. "You and your brother are close, aren't you?"

Jennifer smiled. "We are. We only have each other." She opened a cupboard. "I picked the right one. How many plates? Five?"

"Yup. If Ryan was here, he'd bring one for Rosie too. Did he tell you he made Rosie a hamburger and fed her on a plate the first time I went over to eat with him?"

Jennifer laughed. "He did tell me. And he told me how Rosie sent over dog bone burgers. Should I bring another plate for Rosie?"

"No. She already had dinner. Sometimes I give her some of my crust though. She's really a spoiled dog, but after she saved my life I can never be too good to her."

Daisy yelled from the living room, "What's going on in there? We're hungry. Hurry up and bring out the pizza."

"Okay. Okay. Here we come."

Lily's phone rang. She was annoyed. "Who can that be?" She answered. "Hello? . . . Thanks Elizabeth. I'll be right over."

Lily explained to the others, "I have to run over to the museum. Elizabeth said she found my purse and she'll only be there for another few minutes. Save me some pizza."

Iris offered, "Take my car."

It only took Lily a few minutes to get to the museum. Elizabeth was waiting inside near the floral painting with Lily's purse. "Sorry to make you come now but I need to lock up and I thought you might need this."

"No problem. See you tomorrow?"

"Yes. It's such a shame about Marion but I think she would want us to finish the show." Elizabeth looked toward the back of the museum. "I need to go. Thanks for coming so quickly, Lily."

Lily picked up her purse and looked around the quiet empty museum. It was such a contrast from all the excitement just an hour earlier. A little eerie. A door closed somewhere in the back as Lily walked out the door.

Chapter 4

Ryan knocked on Lily's door early the next morning. Rosie was excited to have company but Lily had been hoping to sleep in. She dragged herself out of bed. "Ryan? What's going on?"

"Can I come in? Something's come up."

Lily was having trouble reading his mood. "Sure. I'll make some coffee."

"Did you go to the museum last night between seven and eight?"

"Come in and sit down."

Ryan was fidgeting and stayed outside. "I'm here on official business, not a social visit."

Lily didn't have a clue what this was all about. "Okay. Come in and we can talk official business then."

Ryan reluctantly sat at her kitchen table. "So, were you at the museum last night?"

She poured two steaming cups of coffee. "Yeah. Elizabeth called me. I forgot my purse and she wanted me to come get it before she left for the night."

Ryan warmed his hands around the coffee cup but didn't pick it up. "Did you see anyone else?"

Lily thought for a minute. "No. I heard a door close when I left, but I didn't see anyone. Why?"

Ryan couldn't look at Lily. "Elizabeth Stevens was found dead this morning. And the painting was stolen." He paused. "The painting that you interpreted with your flower arrangement."

Lily stopped cold. "And?"

Ryan finally looked at Lily. "And. A florist pruning knife was found near the body. The murder weapon. We'll be checking it for prints. Lily, I'm asking as your friend, not a cop. Did you kill Elizabeth Stevens?"

Lily stood up. "Are you serious? You think I killed her?"

"I have to ask. You're the last one who saw Elizabeth."

"Look at me." Lily put her hands on the table and stared at Ryan. "I did not kill Elizabeth Stevens. I picked up my purse. We talked for a minute. She was still very much alive when I left. How do you know someone else didn't come in? Or maybe someone else was already hiding in the museum and killed her after I left? Have you checked the security cameras?"

Ryan looked exhausted and drained. "I don't think you killed her. But there is circumstantial evidence that doesn't look good for you. We haven't finished searching the whole museum. I hope we find some other clues to point us to someone else." Ryan stood up. "The security system was off, maybe as a result of that power outage. I have to go now."

Lily watched him walk out of her kitchen. This felt like a nightmare. Why would anyone kill Elizabeth? She was a sweet, hardworking, dedicated woman. And why would the murderer make it look like Lily was the killer?

There was no chance of getting back to sleep now. "Come on Rosie. Let's take a walk. I need some exercise." Lily attached Rosie's leash and they headed on their loop around town. It was early enough that they could walk without having to stop to chat with anyone. Rosie sniffed all her usual spots and Lily got lost in her thoughts. She made an omelet when she got back and fed Rosie her kibble. Another cup of black coffee and she was wired to get to the shop. "Rosie, you have to stay here. I'll be back at lunch time to let you out." Rosie whined and tried to push through the door with Lily but she had her knee in the way and made Rosie stay inside.

Walking into her shop was instantly calming. Lily took a deep breath. The smell of lavender drifted up from the basket next to the door. She had poured her heart and soul into building up this business and she wasn't going to let anything ruin it. Lily already had several orders on the answering machine for flowers connected to Marion's death. She got busy with those. Work was a good way to forget about her problems until Daisy rushed in with the latest news.

"Have you heard?"

"Heard what?"

Leaning on the work bench, Daisy flattened the front page of the paper for Lily to see. "Elizabeth was murdered at the museum last night. Here's a photo of you next to your arrangement and the floral painting. The painting was stolen. Were you the last one to see her alive?"

Lily grabbed the paper. "I had a bad feeling when Nina wanted to take that photo. Guess who the prime suspect in the murder is?"

Daisy gave Lily a blank stare.

"Does the article say anything about the murder weapon?"

"I don't think so."

Lily slammed her hand on the work bench. "Can you believe it?"

"Believe what? Fill me in."

Lily was all worked up and agitated after reading the article. "Ryan came to my house this morning. He told me I was the last person to see Elizabeth and she was murdered with a florist pruning knife."

"What?"

"He basically said it looks like I'm the murderer."

"If he believes that, why didn't he arrest you?"

Lily picked up some bella donna delphinium and continued working on her arrangement. "He said *he* doesn't think I'm the murderer, but the evidence is pointing to me."

Daisy pulled out her phone. "I'm calling mom. We need to put our heads together and figure out who had a motive to kill Elizabeth."

The bell above the front door jangled as people came into Beautiful Blooms. Some were ordering flowers but others just seemed to be gawking and whispering about Lily since her photo was on the front page of the paper. Misty Valley was small enough that the drama at the museum would be the center of everyone's talk. Tamara Biotchi pushed through to talk to Lily.

With her hands on her hips she glared at Lily and demanded an answer. "What happened last night after everyone left? I heard you went back to the museum and murdered Elizabeth Stevens?"

Lily tried to stay calm. "Tamara, don't believe everything you hear. I did go back to the museum but I can assure you," she looked around her shop, "and anyone else in here who's pretending not to listen, that Elizabeth was very much alive when I left."

Iris arrived with Marigold. "Lily I need to talk to you." She pulled Lily to the design room in the back of the shop, away from prying eyes and ears. Iris got Marigold comfortable in a chair out of the way. Sweet Pea, Lily's resident cat, immediately found Marigold's comfy lap and curled up.

"Marigold overheard some interesting talk last night. Everyone panicked when the lights went out, but of course she didn't know what happened. It's always dark to her but her ears are extra sensitive to make up for what she can't see. I'll let her tell you what she heard."

Daisy called back to Lily that someone needed to speak to her on the phone.

Lily picked up the phone on her desk in the design room. "Hello? . . . No . . . I'm not interested in giving an interview." Lily slammed the phone down. She looked over and saw Iris watching her.

"This is getting so out of control. That was Nina Baldwin. She's covering the murder and wants to interview me. Can you believe it? What does she think, that I'll give her an exclusive on how I killed Elizabeth Stevens?"

"Lily! Don't even talk like that as a joke. Someone might hear you," Iris cautioned.

Lily covered her mouth with her hand. "She really got under my skin. Thanks for bringing me back to reality."

The back door of the shop opened and a head poked in.

Iris and Lily looked at each other confused. "Who is that? Another gawker?"

Lily yanked the door wider. She felt like she was about to boil over with all this chaos surrounding her. "Who are you? What do you want?"

A meek voice answered, "Sorry. I didn't know there was anyone in here."

Lily recognized the girl from last night's opening. "Aren't you Marion Barry's niece?"

The girl nervously looked around and tried to back away from the prying eyes on her. Lily pulled her inside. "What are you carrying?"

The girl clutched a big tote close to her chest, a flat rectangular object inside. "Nothing."

"How about you come in and tell me why you're poking around my shop?"

Her eyes got big. "You're the one on the front page of the paper."

Iris stepped forward. "And you're Maggie, the niece. What are you doing here?"

"I should go."

Iris grabbed her arm. "No you shouldn't. Not until you tell us what's going on."

The tote slipped from her grasp and the corner of a picture frame jutted out.

Lily gasped as she pulled out the floral painting that was stolen from the museum.

"You stole the painting? The police will be interested to know about this." Lily got her phone out.

Maggie pleaded, "Don't call the police. I didn't steal it. I found it."

"Found it? You expect us to believe that?"

"It's the truth. It was outside, in back of the museum. I was looking for a place to hide it until a reward was posted for its return."

Iris looked disgusted. "It's your aunt's painting and you want a reward?"

Maggie hung her head. "I need the money. My brother won't loan me anymore."

Lily found some bubble wrap to cushion the painting and wrapped it securely with an old blanket. "This is going to the police. You'll have to figure out another way to get some money. Maybe you should think about finding a job."

Iris checked on Marigold who just sat quietly, smiling and stroking Sweet Pea. She was happy to be in the middle of the action.

Lily walked to the front of the store to see how Daisy was handling everything there. It had quieted down; it seemed that everyone's curiosity was satisfied, at least for the moment.

"Guess what just walked in the back door?"

Daisy closed the display cooler. "What or who?"

Lily held up her wrapped package. "Marion Barry's niece with the stolen painting. I'm taking it to the police station. Are you all set here until I get back? Mom can help too."

"I'm all set."

Lily went back to get Maggie and bring her along but she had fled out the back door before Iris could stop her. The front door jangled and Lily heard Ryan's deep voice asking Daisy where he could find Lily. He didn't sound happy. Lily walked to the front.

He looked at her package. "What do you have?"

"I was just coming to see you. Marion Barry's niece was sneaking in my back door to try to hide this in my shop." Lily unwrapped the painting and held it up.

Ryan was shocked at what he saw. "I just got an anonymous call that I could find the painting here. But I didn't believe it. Lily, this doesn't look good at all."

The door opened and Nina Baldwin burst in, snapping photos. Of course she got one of Lily holding the painting before Lily had a chance to put it down or shoo Nina from the store.

Nina fired questions at Lily. "Why did you steal the painting, Ms. Bloom?"

Lily's mouth opened and closed without any words coming out. She couldn't believe what was happening. She wondered who kept making her look like a thief and murderer. Her anger fired up her determination to find who was doing this.

Nina turned to Ryan. "I just got an anonymous call that Lily Bloom had the stolen painting. My article will be on the front page again."

Ryan gently took the painting from Lily. He leaned close to her so no one else could hear. "I think you should come to the station so we can talk about this."

Lily started to argue but changed her mind. "Okay. I was coming anyway."

Chapter 5

Lily sat across from Ryan with a pitcher of water and two cups on the table between them. Her brain was trying to organize the events of the last twelve hours. There had to be a logical explanation in there somewhere. Ryan poured water into both cups.

"Lily. Tell me what happened."

"I'm trying to figure it out myself."

"Well, start at the beginning and tell me everything you can remember."

"Elizabeth Stevens introduced me to Marion Barry just before the lights went out. I felt something fall into me, which turned out to be Marion. Is there a cause of death yet?"

"Not yet."

Lily continued. "Ruth Walsh, Marion's personal secretary—have you talked to her?"

"Just tell me the facts and then we'll talk about what I know."

Lily took a sip of water and forced herself to focus. Too much information was twirling around in her head. "Ruth Walsh basically accused me of being the cause of Marion's death." She paused. "It came out of the blue and shocked me." Lily noticed people walking by the room, glancing in. She was glad it was Ryan sitting across from her.

"Nina pulled me away and took some photos. By then, it was like a circus and I left with Daisy, Marigold and my mom."

Ryan was busy scribbling down notes. "Do you remember anything or anyone else that seemed strange?"

"Not really. Elizabeth and her husband were standing together while she announced that the museum was closing."

Ryan looked up. "You went straight home?"

"No. We stopped at the market and I ran in to get some premade pizzas. Then we went to my house. Daisy put the pizzas in the oven and I invited Jennifer over. Nothing out of the ordinary there."

Ryan scowled. "I know you told me some of this before but I want to go over it again to make sure I have it straight. Why did you go back to the museum?"

"We were just about to eat when I got a call from Elizabeth that she found my purse at the museum and could I pick it up. She said she would be leaving shortly but would wait if I came right over."

"What time was that?"

"Um, I guess it was around seven thirty. I drove right over, talked to her for a minute and went back home."

Ryan put his pen down. "Did she seem agitated or upset? Anything out of the ordinary?"

Lily got excited. "Now that you mention it, she did seem distracted. She glanced toward the back of the museum and I heard a door close, so someone else must have been there. At the time it didn't seem unusual, considering what had happened."

"Did you notice if the painting was still there?"

"It was definitely there. She met me right next to the table with my flowers and the painting."

Ryan wrote down more notes, took a sip of water and studied Lily. "Tell me what happened this morning at your shop."

"Well, Maggie, Marion's niece, came in the back door carrying a big tote. She was trying to sneak in and seemed surprised that I was there. She dropped the tote and the painting fell out."

"Why didn't you call me?"

Lily looked down at her sweaty hands on the table. She wiped them on her pants. "I was surprised and was trying to figure out why she had the painting. She said she found it and was hoping for a finder's reward. Can you believe it? Wanting a reward for her aunt's painting? I was about to call you when you arrived."

Ryan nodded. "This all fits together. Apparently someone called me and Nina—I think it was Maggie—about the painting being at your shop."

Lily relaxed a little. "So that's it in a nutshell." Lily sat back and tried to look confident.

Ryan was quiet, thinking. "Do you know the hierarchy at the museum?"

"What do you mean?"

"Obviously before Marion died she was in control. You mentioned her personal secretary, Ruth. Is she in charge now?"

Lily considered this. "I have no idea. I suppose there is a board of directors for that stuff, or maybe her will spells it out."

"I'm trying to get a look at her will. I haven't talked to Ruth yet. I wonder if there was a power struggle between Ruth, the personal secretary, and Elizabeth, the director. Who else would benefit from Elizabeth's death? And why steal the painting?"

Lily got excited. "Daisy heard the niece and nephew gloating that they expect to be millionaires now. That's a motive. Their mother must be in that equation somehow too. Her name is Evelyn Barry Nash. She's much younger than her sister Marion. I think they are all staying at Marion's house. They probably own it now that Marion is dead."

"What about Kirk Stevens? Elizabeth's husband? Do you know anything about him?"

"He owns an antique business in town. Uncommon Antiques. That's about all I know."

Ryan stood up. "Thanks for your help. There are a lot of possibilities to look into. I'll call Nina Baldwin and tell her you found the painting and were turning it over to me so you don't get any more bad publicity over this affair."

"Thanks. So you're not arresting me?"

"Not yet." The corner of his mouth twitched as he tried not to laugh.

Lily followed Ryan to the door. "By the way, your sister is great. She shared a lot last night after we all had a couple of glasses of wine."

Ryan stopped and tensed. "I'm not sure I like the sound of that. Maybe I *will* have to arrest you after all. For twisting her arm."

Ryan walked Lily out. "Oh, there's one more thing." He pulled an envelope out of his pocket. "These were found on the floor around the body." Ryan took Lily's hand and dumped flowers on her palm.

Lily gasped. "Monkshood. These flowers were in the arrangement next to Marion Barry's portrait."

"Do they mean anything?"

She looked up into Ryan's eyes. "The plant is poisonous and can mean danger is near. Some people call it the queen of poisons."

He nodded. "I had a feeling you would know something. I'll add that to my notes."

Ryan watched Lily drive off. She saw him in her rear view mirror. He looked handsome and vulnerable standing in the doorway. At least *he* believed she wasn't involved in the murder. Now she could concentrate on solving the mystery and clearing her name before it affected her business.

Reality hit her smack in the face when she tried to pull into Beautiful Blooms and there wasn't any spot to park. *I hope this is all business*, she thought to herself.

No such luck. TV crews were set up and Nina approached her as soon as her big toe hit the pavement.

"Lily Bloom? Did you kill Elizabeth Stevens?"

She pulled her foot back in the car and slammed her door. She picked up her phone and called Daisy.

"What's going on inside? I'm mobbed out here."

"Crazy here too. Should we close for the day?"

"Yes. Meet me at Mom's house."

It took longer than Lily expected for Daisy, Iris, Marigold and Rosie to show up. But at least when they pulled into the driveway no one was tailing them.

Lily was busy at the kitchen table writing down everyone she thought had a motive. She had to figure this out and get her life back to normal.

Iris was the first to enter the house. "What took you so long at the police station? We were worried you were thrown in jail."

"Not yet. Sit down. We've got work to do. I've got a list of people and we have to do some snooping around." Lily looked up at everyone. "Do you want to help me?" A chorus of yes, of course and definitely, met her ears. "Great."

Iris sat down after she helped Marigold get settled. "First, you have to hear Marigold's story. She was about to tell you before Ryan showed up at the shop."

Daisy interrupted, "No. First, let's have some lunch. I'm starving. What have you got to eat around here, Mom?"

"Look in the fridge. I think I have some left over tortellini and greens. Make a big salad. There's homemade bread in the bread drawer too."

Daisy got busy with that while Marigold told her story. "Well, you all know how my hearing is pretty sharp, right?" Everyone nodded, which was ridiculous since Marigold couldn't see that, but she continued anyway. "I heard two women arguing about who was in charge right after all the commotion started. One reminded me of monkshood and the other had a sweeter voice like a white carnation. The second one was the voice that talked at the end when we all had to leave."

Iris was excited as she looked at Lily. "It must have been that horrible Ruth person who accused you of being the reason Marion died, and Elizabeth. I bet they don't like each other and both want to have control of the museum."

Lily wrote some notes on her paper. She had columns for suspects, motives and clues. "So you think Ruth killed Elizabeth to get control?"

"It's a possibility." Iris sat back with a smug look on her face.

Daisy put a big bowl of tortellini salad in the middle of the table, with plates and forks. "Water?"

Nods again. Iris passed around the plates, filled one for Marigold and one for herself. "Dig in everyone."

Lily remembered about the flowers near the body. "Daisy? Do you remember when we were looking at the arrangement next to the portrait of Marion Barry? Did you notice who made that arrangement?"

Daisy chewed slowly and thought. "I think it was Ruth. Why?"

Lily got busy writing again before she answered. "Ryan told me monkshood blossoms were around the body."

"He knew it was monkshood?" Daisy asked skeptically.

"No. He showed me the flowers and I told him what they were."

Marigold responded. "That can mean danger. And that's the voice I heard. Monkshood. Danger. Ruth."

Chapter 6

Iris announced that they needed to get Tamara Biotchi involved. "I think she's on the board of directors for the museum."

Lily rolled her eyes. "You should have told us that before. She might know who's running the show now."

Iris called Tamara who said she would be over shortly. Ever since her ex-husband and son landed in jail, Tamara broke free from her rigid lifestyle and was up for any adventure. They heard her scooter pull into Iris's driveway just as they finished eating and cleared up the dishes.

Tamara burst into Iris's house, red-faced and wind-blown. "I can't believe I waited so long to enjoy the thrill of riding a scooter. Thank you, Iris, for selling that to me."

Iris teased. "How fast do you go?"

Smiling, Tamara boasted, "I'm up to ten miles an hour."

The others chuckled and Iris said, "You could almost walk that fast. If you think you're having fun now, wait till you get that baby up to forty."

Lily pulled up another chair for Tamara. "We need your help. Are you in?"

Tamara looked around. "I don't know what you got involved in this time but . . . I'm definitely in," she said with a grin from ear to ear.

"Good." Iris asked, "What do you know about what's happening with the museum now?"

"What do you mean? It should open again in a few days. The postponed opening for tonight is cancelled."

"No, how it will be run? Who will have control?"

"Oh, we have an emergency board meeting tonight but I think what will happen is that Evelyn, Marion's sister, will take over Marion's role."

"Which is?"

"She will have final say over who is hired, budget details, that sort of thing."

Lily was busy adding more notes to her columns. "What about Evelyn's kids? Do they fit in at all?"

Tamara thought for a minute. "That's a good question. I'm guessing they'll inherit some of Marion's wealth." She looked around the table. "But that's just a guess. I don't know the details of her will."

"No, I meant are they involved in running the museum at all?"

"Hmmm, I've heard some chatter that Marion's nephew, Jared, would like to be the director."

Iris pumped her fist. "Bingo. He wants Elizabeth's job. The money isn't enough for him. And the niece? She seems like a bit of a loser."

Tamara paused. "I don't like to spread gossip but—"

"But you'd better." Everyone leaned in to hear what was next.

"I've heard she has a drug problem. She's always borrowing money from her mother and brother and they are sick of it."

Iris was pacing around the table. "I'd love to be a fly on the wall at that meeting tonight and hear everything first hand."

Tamara had a devious look on her face. "I found some of those police wire thingies in Tyrone's stuff that he left after the divorce. If we can figure out how to work it, I could wear it and you could listen in. What do you think?"

Everyone cracked up. "Tamara, you never cease to amaze me," Iris shouted. "Get that stuff and we'll figure it out. This is going to be fun. What time is that meeting?"

"I have to be at Marion's house at seven."

Iris checked her watch. "Let's all meet back here at six. That should give us enough time to figure it out. I'll look on YouTube for instructions. You can find anything there."

Lily decided to brave a quick trip back to her shop. With any luck, the media circus would be gone and she could finish up any orders that came in. With her fingers crossed, she turned onto Lupine Lane and was happily met with a deserted, quiet view.

Hopefully my five minutes of fame are over, she thought to herself.

Sweet Pea meowed and rubbed on Lily's leg when she walked in the back door. Lily picked up the little cat. "Are you a little lonely, my little tiger?"

Someone was knocking on the front door. Lily went to the front of the store to see who was so desperate to get in the shop. Kirk Stevens was waiting patiently for her to open the door.

"Hello Mr. Stevens. I'm so sorry about your loss."

He nodded and walked inside. "Thank you. It's quite a shock. I don't think my brain has actually processed what happened to Elizabeth." He looked around. "You have a nice little shop. I don't know why I've never come in before."

Lily put Sweet Pea down and turned her closed sign to open in case there were any other customers in need of flowers. "What can I help you with today?"

He was looking around, studying the buckets of flowers and premade arrangements. "I, ah, need an arrangement."

"Yes?" Lily tried to encourage him to figure out what he wanted.

"Ms. Barry's sister, Evelyn—" He looked up at Lily to make sure she knew who he was talking about. "Evelyn contacted me about having a joint memorial gathering for Marion and Elizabeth."

Lily nodded. "That sounds lovely. When is the gathering?"

"We haven't decided yet. In the next few days I suppose." He leaned over to smell a container filled with lilac.

"Are you thinking about any particular flowers?"

He looked at Lily with eyes filled with tears. "She loved monkshood. Is that something you could get?"

"Monkshood?" Lily was shaken.

He tilted his head and looked carefully at Lily. "Is that a problem? A difficult flower to find?"

She pulled herself together. "It's unusual but I can get some. It's not a flower many people request. I saw that Ruth Walsh used it in her Art in Bloom arrangement of Marion Barry's portrait."

He scowled. "Elizabeth did Marion's portrait arrangement. Ruth was always taking credit for Elizabeth's work. Ruth wanted Elizabeth's job, you know. Elizabeth met her at the museum just before she went home last night to discuss who would take over. I guess she'll get her wish now."

Lily was mentally taking notes to add to her list of suspects and clues. "Ruth was at the museum? What time was that?"

"I'm not sure. I was expecting Elizabeth home around eight so it was sometime before that."

She tried to remain calm. I'm sure that will all get sorted out by the board of directors."

"What do you mean?"

"Nothing really. I just assumed that in a situation like this, the board of directors will figure out how to move forward."

"Yes, I suppose you're right. I just hate to think that Ruth Walsh might get my Elizabeth's job." He sighed. "I'll let you know when the date is decided." He headed toward the door but paused and turned back toward Lily. "I'm thinking about having an opening at my antique shop sometime. I've acquired a lot of new items and would like to encourage more people to come in. Would you be able to do some arrangements for that?"

Lily was caught a little off guard by the timing of the request. "Absolutely. I can't imagine anything nicer than antiques and flowers, except, of course, art and flowers. Bye now." The door jangled as Kirk Stevens departed.

Lily quickly finished putting flowers in the cooler, fed Sweet Pea and gave her another cuddle. "Sorry to be leaving so soon. See you tomorrow."

She drove back to Iris's house, excited to share the new clues Kirk Stevens unknowingly gave her. Tamara and Iris were busy looking through the box of recording stuff that Tamara brought.

"Figure it out yet?"

Iris looked up. "Should be a piece of cake. She can just put this pager size recording device in her purse and we can sit in your van across the street with the receiver."

Lily filled them in about Kirk's visit and the information about Ruth Walsh. "Will she be at the meeting tonight?"

Tamara nodded. "She should be. She was always there in the past, sitting right next to Marion and taking notes. If what you just told us is true, I don't think she'll miss the meeting for anything."

"Who else will be there? I want to make a list so we can figure out the voices."

"Hmmm. Evelyn, maybe her kids, Ruth, Kirk and me."

"Kirk?" Lily was surprised.

"Evelyn decided to invite him out of respect for Elizabeth's death. He doesn't usually come."

Iris was grinning. "Sounds like there might be fireworks with Ruth and Kirk in the same room." She finished fiddling with the recorder. "There. You should be good to go. We'll follow a little later in Lily's van."

Tamara carefully put the recorder in a small pocket in her purse. "This is going to be so exciting. I feel like a real undercover cop." She waddled out the door to her car.

Lily added all the new information to her list before anything slipped from her mind. "Everybody ready to go?"

Iris and Marigold nodded. Daisy asked, "What about Rosie?"

Lily put the leash on Rosie. "She's coming of course." Rosie wriggled with delight. She loved to be included in any adventure.

Lily parked on the street, across and down a bit from Marion's mansion. Tall iron gates guarded the front entrance. They could see Tamara's scooter parked on the circular drive with the other cars.

Iris got the receiver set up and held up the headphones. "All set for the show to start." She exclaimed with glee.

Chapter 7

The ladies sat in the van crowded around the headset. They could hear Tamara's heels tapping along the floor. A loud bang made them all jump. They heard Tamara's voice say, "Oh dear. I dropped my bag." She giggled. "Hope I didn't break anything. Evelyn, your sister's home is beautiful."

"Thank you, Tamara."

A whiny voice piped in. "It's our house now, Mom."

"Not yet, dear. Nothing is official yet."

Iris whispered, "That must be Evelyn's daughter, Maggie. Sounds like a real brat."

Another voice came through the headset. "Let's call this meeting to order. Everyone is here now that Tamara finally decided to honor us with her presence."

Lily looked at the others. "That must be Ruth. I'd remember that nasty voice anywhere."

It sounded like someone slammed a hand on the table. A man's voice said, "Let's get this out in the open right now: Ruth wants Elizabeth's job and I'm against it. She doesn't deserve it after how she treated Elizabeth all these years. And besides, how do we know she didn't kill Elizabeth to get her out of the way once Marion died?"

Gasps came through loud and clear, both through the headset and from the ladies in the van.

"That must be Kirk. He sounds pretty upset," Iris told the others.

Maggie was laughing. "Boy, you know how to cut to the chase. I'm glad I came. This is gonna be a knockdown, drag out power struggle."

Another male voice came through, "Shut up, Maggie. There's no power struggle. Mom's got it all now."

Iris looked at the others and deduced, "That must be the son, Jared."

Finally, Evelyn took control. "Calm down everyone. I know there's a lot of emotions running high tonight but we need to all treat each other with respect. I have a couple of announcements to make. First, I was notified that Marion died of natural causes."

Kirk interrupted, "Yeah, well, it wasn't natural causes that killed Elizabeth."

"Kirk, if you can't be respectful, I'm going to ask you to leave." There were a few seconds of silence. "Okay then. The second item on my agenda is that I would like you, Tamara, to be my interim secretary."

A chair or something crashed, followed by an outburst from Ruth. "I don't believe this. You are all ganging up on me. I dedicated my life to Marion and this museum and this is how you treat me? I don't need to sit here and listen to any more of this outrage." Silence before a door slammed.

The ladies peered out the van window and saw Ruth get into a black sedan and drive like a maniac out of the driveway.

Kirk's voice again. "Good riddance to her. Evelyn, I would like to offer my services as director of the museum."

Jared yelled, "Mom, you know I want that position. This is all so convenient with your sister keeling over and Elizabeth murdered.

I've always wanted to be the director. Don't give it to him just because you feel sorry for him."

All the ladies jumped when they heard a rapping on the driver window. Lily rolled down the window. "Yes, Ryan?"

"What are you doing here parked outside of Marion Barry's house?"

Thinking quickly, Iris told him, "We're waiting for Tamara to finish her meeting."

Ryan looked across the street. "It looks like her scooter is there. What's going on?"

"Nothing," came the innocent answer from four mouths.

He looked at each of them. "Okay then. Get moving."

Lily started the van and headed back to Iris's house. Daisy giggled first. Just a small giggle. But soon they were all laughing uncontrollably. Lily had to pull to the side of the road until she stopped gasping for air. "Did—" Snort. "Did you see—" Snort, snort. "Did you see his face? Okay. That felt good. Anybody hungry? Take out at the Chinese place?"

Iris called in an order once they all decided what they wanted. "We'll pick it up and go back to my house and wait for Tamara."

Lily pulled into the Chinese restaurant. Iris offered to go in and pick up the food. While she was inside, Ruth walked out and looked around as if she was waiting for someone. She got into her car but didn't drive away. Lily was glad she had parked away from Ruth's car so they could watch her without looking suspicious.

Lily was tapping on the steering wheel. "I hope Ruth does something before Iris walks out and she sees the rest of us." Sure enough, Ruth's car door opened and again she glanced around, then threw a big paper bag in the trash.

Daisy looked at Lily. "Want me to go get that bag?"

"Definitely. But wait till she's out of sight."

Just as Iris came out with the food, Daisy ran over to the trash can and grabbed the bag.

Iris stopped and reprimanded her daughter. "Are you that hungry that you have to go dumpster diving?"

Daisy pulled Iris to the van. "Ruth just threw this bag away, we want to see what's in it."

"Probably her Chinese food."

Marigold pointed her finger toward Iris and Daisy climbing in the minivan. "There's death in that bag."

The others were silent, then Lily spoke in a whisper. "What?"

"I can smell it. Death."

Daisy dropped the bag. Iris grabbed it and looked inside. "All I see are dead flowers."

Marigold added. "Monkshood. And something else."

Iris tapped Lily's arm. "Get us back to my house. We'll take a closer look there."

Lily pulled in behind Tamara's scooter. "Uh oh. She's gonna wonder where we've been."

They walked in to find Tamara sitting comfortably on the couch sipping a glass of wine. "Well. Well. Well. You finally made it back." She sat forward and said angrily, "You abandoned me. Where have you been?"

"Calm down, Tamara. Lily's cop friend told us we had to leave." Iris put the take out bag on the coffee table. "We got some food on the way back."

Tamara sniffed the air. "Good idea. I'm starving." She looked at Lily. "What's in that bag?"

Lily glanced down at the bag in her hand. "Oh, Daisy pulled this out of the dumpster."

Tamara grimaced. "Dumpster?"

"We saw Ruth throw it away. She was acting suspicious. We'll look at it after we eat." Lily put the bag by the front door and gave her hands a good scrub.

Iris handed out plates and stuck spoons in all the containers. "Dig in. Fill us in about what happened at the end of the meeting Tamara."

She held up her finger and finished swallowing. "How much did you hear?"

"Jared was yelling at his mother about wanting to be the new director."

"It got weird after that. Kirk walked over to comfort Evelyn. I wanted to disappear. I felt like such an odd man out in that group. Jared got disgusted and left. Maggie kept giggling. Kirk tried to console Evelyn who was crying." Tamara took another bite of food. "No one even seemed to care that I was there. I told Evelyn I would be happy to be her interim secretary." She looked at everyone. "That will keep me in the loop." The others all nodded as they stuffed their mouths with food. "Then I picked up my bag and left."

Lily put her fork down. "Good work, Tamara. You'll be able to let us know what's going on and maybe you can find out about the will too."

Rosie woofed at the sound of a knock on the door.

"Who is it Rosie?" Iris walked over to open the door. "Ryan, nice to see you again. Care to join us for some Chinese takeout?"

He hesitated. "Yeah. Sure. I am hungry." Iris led him into the living room and gave him a plate.

Ryan sat next to Lily and surveyed the group. "This looks interesting." He turned his head to look directly at Lily. "A special occasion?"

Iris shot Tamara a keep-your-mouth-shut glare but she was oblivious and blurted out, "We were just discussing the museum board of directors meeting at Marion's house. Evelyn asked me to be her interim secretary." She puffed up like a peacock, feeling so important with this appointment.

Iris changed the subject, trying to steer the conversation away from their activities. "Ryan, anything interesting happening in Misty Valley tonight?"

"I think so, Iris. That's why I'm here. I thought you ladies might be interested to know the cause of Marion Barry's death." Ryan sat back with a satisfied look on his face.

Tamara piped in. "Oh, we already know. Ouch." Tamara looked at Iris. "Why did you kick me?"

Iris rolled her eyes. "Never mind."

Tamara turned her attention back to Ryan. "It was from natural causes."

Ryan looked puzzled. "Who told you that?"

"Evelyn told us at the meeting."

"That's interesting. I wonder why she said that." Ryan looked slowly at all the ladies staring intently at him. "Marion's death wasn't from natural causes."

Lily gasped first. "It was poison, wasn't it?"

"Why do you say that?"

Lily stood up and paced around the room. "Because of the monkshood—Aconitum—in the arrangement. It's very poisonous."

"It was poison but it hasn't been determined what type yet. Why would someone use a flower in an arrangement if it's so poisonous?"

Lily shrugged. "It's a beautiful flower. Someone must have put some part of the plant in something Marion ate. Maybe Ruth?" Lily remembered the bag on the floor and brought it over to the table. "Let's take a look and see what's in here."

Ryan was surprised. "Is that evidence? Where did you find that?"

Lily put the dead flowers from Ruth's flower arrangement on the table. "We saw Ruth throw it in the trash at the Chinese restaurant." She separated the flowers. "Here's the monkshood."

Ryan looked in the bag and pulled out something else. "Gloves?"

"She probably wore them when she was working with the monkshood." Lily picked one up. "Look at this. It looks like blood on here."

Ryan carefully gathered everything and put it all back in the bag. "I'm going to take this. It could be important."

Chapter 8

Lily decided to visit Kirk's antique shop before opening Beautiful Blooms the next morning. If he asked her to make arrangements for his opening, she wanted to know what the setting would be like. He was located off Main Street in an old brick building. The big oak front door had an antique iron door knob. She walked in to a light filled interior with exposed beams and wide pine flooring.

"Good morning Lily." She looked to her left, following the sound of a deep voice greeting her. "What a nice surprise. What can I do for you?"

"Just looking around. You have exquisite antiques. Where does it all come from?"

Kirk smiled. "I get a lot of items from estate sales. Sometimes, someone calls me with a few pieces to sell." He walked over to a table with an urn on it. "Like this, for example. A young lady came in recently with a few pieces she wanted to sell quickly."

Lily's jaw dropped. "That urn belongs to my mother. Who sold it to you?"

Kirk was insulted. "I can't reveal my sources. I'm sure you're mistaken. It could *look* like an urn your mother has but I can assure you, it isn't hers."

Lily opened the top. "What is this inside?"

Kirk's face visibly blanched. "I . . . I don't know."

"I'll tell you what it is. It's my father's ashes. What else did that young woman bring in? Who was it? Maggie Nash?" Lily said with disgust. "I think Ryan Steele will be very interested in this." Lily pulled her phone from her pocket.

Kirk held her arm. "Please don't call the police. I'll give this to you. Take it. I don't want any bad publicity."

"Are you crazy? I can't do that. Lots of people in town have had antiques stolen recently and you're profiting from that. I can't believe it." Lily picked up the urn and stomped out to her minivan. She drove straight to the police station after she called Iris to tell her she had the urn.

Lily ran into the station looking for Ryan. She almost crashed into him as he was about to walk out. "Slow down, Lily. Where's the fire?"

"No fire, but look at this." She held up the urn.

"You found it? Where?"

"At Uncommon Antiques. Kirk didn't want me to tell you but I bet he has more of the stolen items."

Ryan took the urn and carefully placed it on his desk. "Did he steal it?"

"He told me that a young lady sold a few things to him. I bet it's Maggie Nash."

"Sit down and take a deep breath before you hyperventilate. Tell me why you think it's Maggie." Ryan placed the urn on his desk and steered Lily to a chair.

She put her head in her hands until her breathing was back to normal and she could explain her theory. "Don't you remember? She had that stolen painting from the museum she was trying to hide in my shop. Tamara told me she has a drug problem. I bet she stole the antiques and then sold them to Kirk for drug money."

Ryan put his hat on. "I'm going over to Uncommon Antiques to have a look around. Why don't you take that back to your mother's house where it belongs? By the way, are the ashes still inside?"

Lily took the lid off. "See? Still here. Shouldn't that have been a clue to Kirk?

"Lily?"

She looked at Ryan, waiting for him to continue.

"I told the lab about the monkshood and they're checking for aconitine, the poison in the monkshood plant. You need to be careful with all this poking around you always do. And tell your friends too. There is a killer out there. Maybe two."

Lily leaned against the desk and watched Ryan leave. She picked up the urn, gave it a hug and silently said hello to her father, then called Iris. "Mom? Meet me at the shop."

Daisy and Iris were peeking out the back door anxiously waiting for Lily. They both had huge smiles when she walked in with the urn.

Iris reached out first. "Let me hold it. I've missed having Dad keep me company." She looked at the two girls. "Don't look at me like I'm crazy. I know it's not really him but it's the thought of him that I like having around."

Lily hugged her mom. "I don't think you're crazy. I was talking to Dad on the drive over. It is a comfort to have him back."

Daisy nodded in agreement. "I think we're all together on this and I don't care if anyone thinks we're crazy."

The front door jangled. Iris sat in the chair in the workshop holding the urn and looking like she was lost in her memories. Lily whispered to Daisy. "Let her be. Mom and Dad were such a perfect team. I hope I find that someday."

"Me too," Daisy said with a sad look on her face.

The front door slammed closed. "Hello? Hello? Anyone here?"

Lily headed toward the front of the shop. "Hi Jennifer. Is something wrong?"

Jennifer was holding the hand of a young girl who was clutching a well-loved teddy bear. "I hate to bother you, Lily." She looked down at the girl. "I have a huge favor to ask."

Lily glanced from Jennifer to the girl, trying to figure out what was happening. Jennifer looked distraught and the girl was trying to hide behind Jennifer's legs.

"Okay."

"My ex-husband dropped Katie off first thing this morning. I can't get hold of Ryan and I have to go to court." Jennifer picked Katie up. "Could you watch her for the morning? I don't know anyone else in town to ask."

Lily's mouth fell open. *What will I do with a little girl? She doesn't look much more than five years old.* She panicked.

Iris came out holding Sweet Pea.

Katie's eyes got huge and she whispered to her mom, "Can I pat the kitty?"

Iris walked over to Katie who was squirming to get down. Jennifer smiled as Iris put Sweet Pea in Katie's arms. She cuddled the cat whispered in its ear. Iris looked at Jennifer. "I think she'll be fine here. We'll be in the design room if you need us," she said over her shoulder to Lily as she guided Katie to the back. "Come on Katie. I think Sweet Pea is waiting for her breakfast."

Katie looked up in awe at Iris. "Can I feed her?"

"Of course. We were waiting for you to come just for that reason." Iris winked at the others.

"Really?"

"Really, honey. Say goodbye to your mom. She'll be back in a jiffy."

Katie happily followed Iris. "Bye Mom."

Lily was stunned. "What just happened?"

Jennifer laughed. "Iris knows girls. Look at what a great job she did with you and Daisy."

"Well—"

Jennifer cut off whatever story Lily thought she should share. "I'll let Ryan know that Katie is here and if he has time to come and get her. I'm not sure when I'll be back but hopefully it won't be too late. How can I ever thank you?"

"It will be fine. Iris needs something to do to keep her out of my hair. If Katie gets bored with Sweet Pea, we can always get Rosie. She loves kids."

Jennifer's eyes were about to spill over. "Here's my number. Just in case. Thanks again."

Lily shooed Jennifer out of the shop, then peeked in the back room and watched Katie hovering over Sweet Pea while she ate. Iris quietly sat nearby, probably still daydreaming about times gone by. Daisy was busy making arrangements.

The doorbell jangled, bringing Lily back to the present. "Can I help you?"

"I hope so. I'm Evelyn Nash."

"Evelyn. I'm Lily Bloom. I don't think we met before but I met your sister. What a wonderful woman she was, and so generous in supporting programs in Misty Valley."

"Thank you, Lily. I'm going to miss her terribly." She fidgeted, picking up flowers and absentmindedly smelling them. "You have a charming shop. It feels so calming standing here amongst all the flowers." She took a deep breath. "And the smell. What is that? I can't place it."

"Probably the lilac you're standing next to. Lots of people don't think to use it as a cut flower so they don't recognize the sweet smell when it's inside." Lily put her hand on Evelyn's arm. "I loved the portrait of your sister and the arrangement that Elizabeth did with the monkshood. It was striking."

Evelyn looked confused. "Elizabeth's arrangement? With the monkshood? No, that was Ruth Walsh."

"Oh, Kirk told me Elizabeth made it. In any case, it was unusual and effective."

"About Ruth—"

"Yes?"

Evelyn furtively looked around and lowered her voice to barely a whisper. "I think she might have poisoned my sister."

Lily looked horrified. "I heard it was natural causes." She crossed her fingers for lying about this but wanted to hear what else Evelyn wanted to tell.

Evelyn was surprised to hear this. "You did?"

"Yes. Tamara told me. I hope that doesn't get her in trouble."

"No. I told everyone at the meeting it was natural causes so Ruth wouldn't think anyone suspected her."

Lily took a gamble with the next question, trying to sound casual. "What will happen with the museum now?"

"My sister left it all to me. At least that's what she told me. I'll find out the exact details later today when the lawyer goes over the will with me."

"Do you have anyone in mind to be the new director?"

Evelyn laughed. "Are you after the job too? It seems that everyone wants to be director. Between you and me, I'll probably hire my son, Jared. But don't tell Kirk Stevens. He can have a temper when he doesn't get his way."

Lily studied the immaculate look that Evelyn presented. A light blue linen skirt, white silk blouse and comfortable sandals. She was tall. Taller than Lily, and held her body regally, like a statue. It made it hard for Lily to read her body language.

"When did you know it was poison?"

"I suspected it from the very beginning but I don't have any proof."

"I'm sure the police will sort it all out and let you know when they have any information."

"I suppose you're right." Evelyn shook her head as if to get rid of those morbid thoughts. "I almost forgot. The reason I'm here is to order some flowers for a memorial gathering Kirk Stevens and I are planning for his wife, Elizabeth, and my sister, Marion." Evelyn paused and looked carefully at Lily. "We decided to do it together. At the museum."

Lily picked up her notebook. "Okay. What did you have in mind?"

Evelyn looked around the shop. "I'm thinking a big colorful bouquet for the entryway. Blues, pinks, white and greens. And another big bouquet filled with garden flowers—lilies, snapdragons, sweet William, and dahlias—for the main gallery. I have two beautiful antique vases for the arrangements."

Lily made some notes. "When is the memorial?"

"Tomorrow night." She paused, thinking. "I'd like you to come. Keep an eye on Ruth. See if she says anything or acts oddly. Oh, and bring your mother and sister if they want to come."

Lily tried not to look surprised about the invitation. "I'd be happy to come." *This is perfect,* she thought. *We won't need to have Tamara wired this time. We can all watch and listen.*

Chapter 9

Iris and Katie were walking back to Lily's house for some lunch and to visit with Rosie. The two were deep in conversation when Ryan's police car pulled up next to them.

"Uncle Ryan, Uncle Ryan! I got to feed Sweet Pea this morning," Katie announced with pride.

Ryan smiled. "Aren't you lucky? Where are you two lovely ladies going?"

"Katie and I are going for some lunch until Jennifer gets back. Care to join us?"

"I'd love to. I have about a half hour. Bring Rosie and I'll have lunch ready for you."

Katie skipped along the sidewalk without a care in the world. She stopped and gave Iris a very serious look. "Do you think I could get a kitty?"

Iris laughed. "You'll have to ask your mom. But if she says yes, I know just the place to go. Here we are. Do you want me to take you into Uncle Ryan's house before or after I let Rosie out?"

"After, after. I want to meet Rosie." Katie jumped up and down with excitement. A cat and a dog in the same day. She acted like she'd won the lottery.

Iris opened the door to an extremely excited Rosie. She had never met a person she didn't like. Except, of course, if that person was trying to hurt Lily. And the smaller the better. Rosie licked Katie and wiggled all over. Rosie ran around the back yard in circles with Katie trying to keep up. Iris watched and laughed. She saw Ryan standing on his back deck watching too.

Iris joined Ryan next door. "I just want to warn you, Katie will want a cat or dog after today's adventures."

Ryan smiled. "I was thinking that might just be exactly what she needs. I never told you and Lily why Jennifer is staying with me. I was waiting for her to share that story. The short version is that she had to get away from an abusive situation. Her ex was so jealous and paranoid, she couldn't stay with him any longer. She's in court today to try to get sole custody."

Iris nodded and waited for Ryan to continue if he wanted to.

"She will be living with me for a while. Until she can get back on her feet." He watched Katie and Rosie play a dog version of tag. "I'm glad she's happy with you today. Jennifer will need a lot of help."

Katie was screaming with delight as Rosie brought sticks for her to throw. Iris nodded. "Raising kids is not a one person job. She's a joy. I'll be happy to help in any way I can. My girls aren't producing any grandkids, so I'll have to adopt someone else's," she said with a twinkle in her eye.

Ryan called to Katie, "Don't wear out Rosie. Come on up and get some lunch before I have to go back to work." He turned to Iris. "I had an interesting visit with Kirk at Uncommon Antiques. I warned Lily already and I want to repeat the warning to you: there's at least one, maybe two killers out there. Don't do anything foolish."

"Who, me? I'm just a little old lady. Whatever could I do to get into trouble?" she said with sarcastic sincerity. "Did you find more stolen antiques in his shop?"

Ryan reached down and picked up Katie, swinging her around and around while she squealed with pleasure. "I sure did. He's got a lot of explaining to do."

Katie screeched. "Don't stop. Don't stop."

Laughing, Ryan set Katie down. "I have to eat and get back to work. What are you doing after lunch?"

Katie ran to the table and started eating a sandwich like she hadn't eaten in days. In between bites, she managed to tell Ryan the plan. "Iris is taking me to meet her friend Marigold." Another bite. "Marigold can't see anything with her eyes. Iris told me Marigold sees with her fingers and ears." She looked at Ryan in total seriousness. "I want her to teach me how to do that too."

Ryan patted her on the head. "I'm sure you'll have a good time with Marigold and Iris. See you later."

Iris finished her sandwich and cleaned up the dishes. "Let's throw the stick a few more times for Rosie, then go visit Marigold."

***

Beautiful Blooms was hectic all morning; people in and out for orders of small bouquets to huge arrangements. Lily barely noticed Maggie lurking around in the background until everything quieted down. Maggie made her way closer to Lily after the door closed on the last customer.

"I need to talk to you." Maggie was hunched over looking at the floor.

"Come on in the back." Maggie followed Lily like a whipped puppy. Lily motioned for her to sit in the chair. Sweet Pea jumped on her lap and curled up. Lily asked, "What's going on?"

Maggie stroked Sweet Pea. Her shoulders relaxed and she sighed. "Did you tell the police that I sold stolen antiques to that creep Kirk Stevens?"

Lily was caught completely off guard. "Not in those words. Why?"

"The police have been asking my mom a lot of questions about me and she read me the riot act." She looked at Lily with alligator tears in her eyes. "I didn't steal that painting and I didn't steal any antiques."

Lily sat down next to Maggie, trying to seem less threatening and wondering if the alligator tears were real or an act. "Kirk told me that a young lady sold him the antiques. I thought it might be you."

"Everyone *always* thinks it's me just because I did drugs." She gave Lily a long hard look. "I'm off drugs. I've been clean for a while."

Lily waited patiently sensing there was something else Maggie wanted to get off her shoulders.

"Everyone thinks Jared, my brother, is perfect. Mom always compares me to him. She assumes he never does anything wrong. Ya know what I think?" Maggie looked up again.

Lily answered, "Jared's the one who stole the antiques?"

Maggie shrugged. "That's what I think. Kirk wouldn't rat on him and get Mom upset. That weasel is trying to stay on Mom's good side. Jared probably stole the painting too. He didn't care about Aunt Marion. He's happy she's out of the way so he can work his way into running the museum."

The front door jingled. Daisy went to see who came in.

Lily wanted more information from Maggie. "What do you think your mother will do?"

"I don't know. I think she's torn between Jared and Kirk. My guess? Jared will win out. He's always been Mom's favorite."

Ryan walked into the design room. Maggie stiffened up again and her face took on a blank look. Lily left her with Sweet Pea and motioned for Ryan to follow her outside.

Ryan eyed Lily. "What's with her? Trying to steal something from your store?"

Lily put her finger to her lips. "Shhhhh. She just told me she thinks Jared is the one who stole the painting and the antiques. Did you find out anything from Kirk Stevens?"

"Lots of stolen antiques. Of course, he said he had no idea those antiques were stolen. That guy is slick and he's hiding something." He changed the subject. "I had a nice lunch with Katie and your mom. Katie seems to be completely comfortable with Iris. Thanks for helping Jennifer out."

"It wasn't me. It was all Mom. She stepped right in with Sweet Pea and that's all it took to distract Katie."

"Oh yeah, Sweet Pea. Katie asked me if she can get a kitten." Ryan laughed. "I think it's a good idea. What do you think?"

Lily smiled. "You're asking me? I'd have every cat and dog that needs a home if I had the room. Definitely a good idea."

Maggie interrupted Lily and Ryan's conversation when she walked out the back door. "There's going to be a memorial gathering, as my Mom calls it, for Marion and Elizabeth. Tomorrow at the museum. You should come. I think there will be some fireworks. And not the fourth of July type." She left without looking back.

Lily watched her walk off. "I wonder what she's referring to." Lily asked Ryan.

"We'll just have to go and find out. Do you believe what she told you?"

Lily scrunched up her mouth in thought. "She's no dummy. She has low self-esteem and a lack of confidence but I think she's an observer and she probably has a good perspective on what's going on with her family dynamics. I do believe her. It doesn't seem like she has anything to gain by lying to me."

"Unless she's the murderer."

"Well, there is that I suppose."

Ryan changed the subject. "I got a message from Jennifer and she wants to make dinner for you, Iris, Daisy and Marigold for helping her out with Katie today. My house around six?"

"That's very nice. We'll be there. I'll bring a salad, okay?"

Ryan's police pager went off. His face got serious. "I have to go to the hospital. Someone tried to run Ruth Walsh off the road."

Chapter 10

Ryan's house smelled delicious when Lily walked in with a big salad. Iris arrived with Marigold and fresh bread and Daisy brought brownies. Katie jumped up and down, excited to see her new friends. She hugged Rosie and ran with her to the backyard.

Jennifer was smiling and humming as she got dinner ready. Jennifer looked up at Lily. "Katie told me that she had a good time today. You all have been wonderful to her."

Lily watched Rosie and Katie playing. "How did it go in court today?"

Jennifer took the eggplant parmesan out of the oven, placing it on the island to let it cool. "It went well. It looks like the judge is going to grant me sole custody. My ex has been completely unreliable with his responsibilities with Katie. I know he loves her and he can still visit but she needs a routine she can depend on and he wasn't being responsible about that."

Screaming broke up their conversation. Lily ran outside to see Katie on the ground holding her arm. Jennifer ran straight to Katie and picked her up. "What's wrong sweetie?"

"My arm. My arm."

Everyone else was on the deck in seconds. Iris took charge. "Get in my car. I'll take her to the emergency room."

Jennifer climbed into the back of Iris' VW holding the screaming child. Lily told Rosie to get in the back too and Lily got in the passenger seat. Rosie put her head on Katie's lap and the screaming subsided to deep sobs. Daisy and Marigold followed Iris to the hospital.

Jennifer stroked Katie's head. "You'll be okay. What happened?"

Sob. Sob. Hiccup. "I fell off the big rock."

Iris pulled into the emergency drop off area. "Here we are. Take Katie in and I'll park."

Jennifer carried Katie inside while Iris pulled her car into the parking lot. Lily saw Ruth Walsh walking through the parking lot. "Stop here. Let me out. I want to talk to Ruth."

Lily jumped out of the car and called, "Ruth. Ruth."

Ruth turned toward Lily but kept on walking.

Lily ran to catch up. "Can I talk to you for a minute?"

Ruth had her hand on her car door. "What do you want?"

"I was hoping we could talk about the museum. You must know more than anyone else."

"Know what?" she asked with disgust.

"Well, how it's run. Who Marion was leaving it all too?"

Ruth opened her door. "What is it to you?"

"Listen Ruth. I don't know why you dislike me so much. I'm just trying to figure out what happened to Marion and Elizabeth. And the way you have been acting, lots of people think you had something to do with it."

This got Ruth's attention. She turned with her mouth open and her eyes wide. "Me? Are you serious?"

Lily nodded her head.

"That's the most ridiculous thing I've ever heard. I've dedicated my life to that museum and to Marion Barry. She was like a mother to me. I would never harm a hair on her head." Tears were streaming down her cheeks.

Lily patted her shoulder. "I'm sorry. How about we find someplace quiet to talk a little more?"

Ruth blew her nose and wiped the tears from her face. "Okay."

Lily led Ruth to a small outside garden with benches. "How is this?"

Ruth sat on a bench next to a small gurgling pool. Goldfish swam around and a couple of frogs sat on rocks at the edge of the water. She looked at Lily. "I don't know why I was so mean to you after Marion died. I think I was in shock and a little jealous that you were there for her and I wasn't."

Lily sat down next to Ruth. "Did you know that Marion was murdered? It wasn't natural causes like Evelyn told everyone at the meeting."

Ruth turned white as a sheet. "Murder? Why would anyone murder that dear old lady?"

"That's what I'm trying to figure out. Someone made me look guilty and someone has been trying to make you look guilty. And now someone tried to run you off the road? Can you think of any reason for all this?"

Ruth scraped the toe of her shoe in the dirt under the bench. "Her will." Lily waited and Ruth continued. "Marion was going to make an announcement at the opening. Elizabeth and I were the only ones who knew ahead of time." Ruth looked at Lily. "I was her personal secretary for the last twenty years and she always confided in me."

"What was the announcement?"

Ruth looked at the goldfish swimming in the pond. "She had decided to change her will and donate the Misty Valley Museum to the town of Misty Valley with a trust fund for the overhead expenses. She thought it would be nice to announce it at the opening with so many of the town people in attendance."

"Who was getting the museum before the change?"

Ruth sounded disgusted. "Evelyn of course. She was never interested in the museum like Marion was. The museum was like a child to Marion. She put all her love and energy into it." Ruth looked over at Lily. "I understood that, but Evelyn just saw it as a way to get rich. Her and her greedy kids."

"Was the will already changed before the opening?"

"I don't know if she had signed it. I think she wanted to discuss it with Evelyn first. I tried to tell her that was a bad idea but she had her mind made up. She could be very stubborn at times."

Silence hung between them for a few minutes. Lily walked around the garden. "Ruth? Why did you throw away that flower arrangement and gloves after the board of directors meeting?"

Ruth angrily stood up. "Were you spying on me?"

"No. I was waiting for my mother to get take out when you came out."

"You took that bag out of the trash?"

Lily hung her head guiltily. "Yes. You were acting suspicious."

"I don't know why I even agreed to talk to you." Ruth hustled off to her car.

Lily watched her drive off, then went into the hospital to see how Katie was doing. She found Iris, Daisy and Marigold in the waiting area. "Any news about Katie?"

Ryan walked over to the ladies. "The doctor thinks she broke her arm. They have to do x-rays. I can stay here if you want to go back home."

Lily pulled Ryan aside. "I had an interesting chat with Ruth. There's something odd about her. Did you find out anything?"

"We can talk about it later."

Iris got up. "Tell Katie she's a brave girl and Sweet Pea will be waiting for her tomorrow morning."

Ryan smiled. "Thanks Iris. I'm sure that will make her happy."

Lily helped Marigold get up and they went to the parking lot to drive home. Marigold had been quiet through the whole ordeal but piped up now. "That little girl is just like a climbing clematis."

"What do you mean?"

"She winds her way into our hearts."

Lily and Daisy nodded. Iris smiled. "You just hit the nail on the head with that description. Now, let's dig into that eggplant parmesan. No use letting it go to waste." Iris slammed her door and got her VW moving with Daisy having trouble keeping up.

The back door of Ryan's house was open. Lily looked at the others. "Did we leave in such a hurry, we forgot to close the door?"

Iris barged inside. "Thank goodness no one stole the eggplant parmesan. Let's take all the food to your house, kick back and Lily can fill us in about Ruth."

Iris got it all organized. "Dig in. I'll get a plate for Marigold."

Lily fed Rosie before she got herself some food. "I didn't realize how hungry I am. This looks delicious. Ryan will be eating well if Jennifer sticks around."

A pounding on the back door startled everyone and got Rosie barking ferociously. Lily put her plate on the coffee table and peered out the back door to see an unknown face scowling at her.

She held Rosie's collar to keep her from charging at the man standing there.

Just opening the door a crack, she asked, "Can I help you?"

Without any greeting, he spit out, "Where's my daughter? What did that no good ex-wife of mine do with her? She's not taking her away without a fight." He tried to push the door open but Rosie snarled and lunged at him. "Tell her I'll be back."

Lily slammed and locked the door. Iris grabbed her purse. "I'm going back to the hospital to warn Ryan and Jennifer. She can stay at my house. He won't know to look for her there." She turned to Lily. "Can Marigold stay here?"

"Of course. Do you want Daisy to go with you?"

"I'll be fine." She patted her purse. "I've got protection with me."

Rosie darted through the door and waited by Iris' car. Lily told Iris, "Rosie wants to go with you. She can keep Katie company."

Lily smiled but also felt fear. She knew Iris never backed down from a challenge and it got her into some difficult situations at times.

Lily watched as Iris drove away. She didn't notice a car following a few minutes later.

Chapter 11

Lily opened one eye to see fog as thick as pea soup out the window. She pulled the soft comforter over her head and thought it would be nice to sleep until ten. Unfortunately, that wasn't going to happen. She threw the comforter off. Something hot like a shower and something else hotter like a cup of hazelnut coffee would get her blood moving. As she pulled on her low rise jeans she realized all those sweets were creating a bit of a muffin top. *Note to self, cut out the carbs—well, start tomorrow,* she thought as she spied the last blueberry muffin calling to her from the counter. With muffin, coffee and tote in hand, she checked that Marigold was all set and she headed out for the shop.

Lily kicked her door closed and heard a voice. "Hi neighbor."

Her juggling act failed as coffee splashed onto her formerly clean, yellow t-shirt. "Ryan. We never got a chance to talk last night. What was the deal with Ruth?" she asked as she looked down at the stain.

"Do you need some help?"

"Only if you have a clean t-shirt in your pocket," she said as she tried to mop up the stain only to make it worse. "Wait here, I have to change."

"Do you need help with that?" he teased.

Lily was right back looking fresh as a daisy and they walked down the driveway together. "Ruth claims someone tried to run her off the road. She got a few scrapes when her car hit the guardrail but she didn't get the plate number. She said it might be a Honda. Do you know how many Hondas are out there?"

"She told me something interesting."

Ryan waited patiently. "Oh?"

"She said Marion Barry was going to change her will and give the museum to the town of Misty Valley with a trust fund for overhead expenses."

"Really? That might upset someone."

"Exactly what I was thinking. Probably Evelyn. By the way, how's Katie?"

Ryan opened the minivan door for Lily. "She's fine. She has a cast, but it was a clean break so it should heal quickly. What happened with Jennifer's ex?"

"What a creep. He pounded on my door looking for Katie. Was Jennifer worried?"

"Very. He is unpredictable. It was nice of Iris to let them stay with her."

Lily slid into the seat of her minivan. "Another busy day. See you tonight at the museum?"

"I'll be there."

Lily was happy to hear that. She was hoping to spend more than five minutes with Ryan. There was something about him that made her feel different. A good kind of different. Lily backed out and drove to the shop.

Evelyn was already outside Beautiful Blooms waiting for Lily.

"Good morning, Evelyn. What can I do for you?" Lily unlocked the front door and held it open for Evelyn to walk in.

"Nothing good about this morning. I can't believe it."

"Believe what?"

Evelyn was beside herself. "My sister. She changed her will. She left the museum to the town. I think Ruth Walsh was behind this. I need your help."

Lily moved flowers from the cooler to the front of the shop. "I don't know how I can help."

"Watch her like a hawk tonight at the memorial. See if she tries to sneak into the office."

Lily stopped and looked at Evelyn. "How can you be sure she will even come?"

"She'll be there. I told her there was something for her in the will and I would give it to her tonight."

"Maybe you should have the police come."

Evelyn shook her head. "I don't want to be that obvious.

Lily finished the bouquet she had been working on. "How is this for the entryway? Colorful enough?"

"Yes. Beautiful. What is that green flower?"

"Bells of Ireland. Green is popular now. When will you be at the museum for the delivery?"

"I'll be there all day. Come anytime."

A siren broke into the peacefulness of the shop. Daisy ran in looking terrified. "Have you heard?"

Lily got worried. "Heard what?"

"Jennifer's ex-husband tried to break into Mom's house. Rosie knocked him down and guarded him while Mom called 911."

Evelyn looked horrified. "Who is Jennifer?"

Lily was barely able to reply. "Ryan Steele's sister. Her ex-husband came to my house yesterday looking for her and her daughter, Katie. We thought they would be safe at Iris' house."

Daisy was pacing around. "Come on. We need to go to Mom's house."

Lily stared out the car window. "I can't believe this." She looked back at Daisy. "Good thing Mom took Rosie."

Daisy pulled into Iris' driveway. There were police cars everywhere. The normally quiet street was anything but at the moment.

Jennifer was sitting on the couch with her arms wrapped around Katie. Rosie was curled up next to them. Lily patted Rosie and put her hand on Jennifer's shoulder.

Jennifer didn't move. "I don't know how he found us here. I should have known."

"There's no way to know something like this. He was determined to find Katie."

Jennifer finally looked at Lily. "Rosie protected her. How did she know?"

Lily shrugged. "Rosie just knows these things. She makes me feel safe."

Iris walked in from the kitchen and clapped her hands. "Who's ready for some pancakes? The first batch is ready. I have real maple syrup too. Made right here in Misty Valley at the Misty River Farm."

Katie jumped up. "I'm hungry. I want some." Rosie stayed by her side.

Iris ushered her into the kitchen. "Great. Climb into the chair. You get the first ones. Do you think Rosie wants one too?"

Katie looked at Rosie staring intently her. "Yes. She just told me she *does* want a pancake."

Lily tactfully asked Jennifer about her ex while they were out of Katie's earshot. "What will happen now?"

Jennifer shook her head. "Ryan said he'll be in jail for a while. I won't have to worry about custody." She looked up at Lily. "I still can't believe this."

"Shake it off and get some pancakes with Katie. I'm heading back to my shop."

The arrangement for the museum was still on the work bench. Lily put it in the cooler and got out more flowers—lilies, delphinium, snapdragons and greens—for the next bouquet.

Tamara burst into the shop with her normal whirlwind of energy. The door slammed behind her.

"Is Iris alright?" she hollered to Lily.

Lily walked to the front. "Yeah. Rosie saved the day again. It was weird. Last night when Iris left my house, Rosie insisted on going too. That dog has a sense when danger is around."

Tamara plopped into the chair. Lily tried not to wince wondering if the chair would hold Tamara's bulk or shatter, dropping her to the floor. The chair survived. "What happened?" Tamara always wanted to know all the gossip.

Lily filled her in on the details of Jennifer, Katie and the ex-husband.

Tamara grimaced and declared emphatically, "You don't have to tell me about ex-husbands. Don't I know all about *that*."

Lily chuckled. "I guess you are a bit of an expert. By the way, are you going to the museum memorial tonight?"

"Of course. Evelyn said she needs me there to help her keep track of all the guests." Tamara lowered her voice. "She's distraught over what she found out in the will. I'm not supposed to tell anyone. But—"

"But?"

"Okay. As long as you don't repeat any of this." Tamara looked around the empty shop, expecting to see someone hiding in the corner. "Evelyn's sister changed the will and is leaving the museum to the town."

"Interesting. You're the third person I've heard this from."

Tamara's face got red and she stuttered, "You . . . you already know this?"

"Ruth and Evelyn told me. It doesn't seem to be that big of a secret."

"And, it was stated that Elizabeth could stay on as the director for as long as she wanted the position."

Lily perked up. "That's interesting. I hadn't heard that part yet. So who will be the new director?"

Tamara shook her head. "I wish I knew. But it definitely won't be Ruth."

Lily paused. "Did you actually *see* the will?"

"Well, no. Why?"

"Just wondering."

The front door jingled and both women looked up. Lily smiled at the sight of Ryan walking in. She felt her heart beat a little faster.

Tamara pushed herself upright with a grunt. "Well, I think I'll go see how Iris is holding up. See you tonight Lily."

Ryan moved aside so Tamara could get out the door without knocking into anything. "Lily, I don't know how to thank you." He strode toward her and embraced her in a big bear hug. "I could never forgive myself if something happened to Jennifer or Katie," he whispered into her hair while holding her tightly.

Lily could only think how good it felt to have Ryan's strong arms around her. She melted into him, wishing this moment would never end. He smelled good, like leather and maleness. She was barely breathing. She stepped back a little so she could look into his dark eyes. "I'd like to take credit, but I didn't do anything."

"You sent Rosie home with Iris. How did you know?"

"Rosie knew. I just let her follow her instincts. She sensed danger and wanted to go with Iris."

He pulled her close again. "I'm going to make Rosie a deputy if she keeps saving people like this."

Lily snorted. "Will she get to wear a uniform?"

They both started to laugh. "Maybe a vest so we have someplace to pin her badge."

"Well, you can't have her. I need her around to keep me safe."

Ryan looked at her carefully. "That's a good idea. I want you to be safe, too." He leaned in so quickly, Lily wasn't even prepared for his lips on hers. But it didn't take more than a second to recover and enjoy the feeling.

The door jingled. Lily jumped and moved away from Ryan.

Daisy was standing behind them with a devious grin on her face. "Is this Beautiful Blooms Flower Shop or did I walk into the wrong shop?"

Lily's face was burning.

Ryan was smiling and looking happy. "Oh, I thought this was the Beautiful Bloom Women Shop." He looked at Lily. "I found the one I want."

Daisy laughed out loud. "Lily, pull yourself together. You just got the compliment of your life. Are you speechless?"

Ryan gave her another quick hug. "It's okay. Speechless says it all." Another smile. "I have to get back to work."

Lily was frozen in place watching Ryan disappear out the door.

"Earth to Lily. He'll be back. Don't worry."

Lily's face broke into a big goofy smile. "I wasn't expecting that."

Daisy looked in the cooler. "Do you have the museum order ready to go?"

"Ummm, almost."

Daisy shook her head. "Looks like you haven't even started on the second one. Better get your head back into flower world."

Lily looked at the flowers she had on the bench and it was like a bell went off. "Oh, I'll finish this and we can take them to the museum. Evelyn said she would be there all day."

Daisy made up a few cash and carry bouquets and put them in the display cooler. They usually flew out of the shop. People always popped in and loved to look at what was in the cooler. The hottest sellers lately were pink alstroemeria with yellow gerbera daisies and a sprig or two of greens. Calla lilies were also popular. All they needed was a little green like hosta leaves to accentuate the pure white.

Lily examined her arrangement. It had a nice airy look to it, like a garden with tall white lilies, dainty blue bella donna delphinium, bold yellow and pink snapdragons and various ornamental grasses.

"I'm ready to go. Let's get these into the van and find Evelyn. She said she has her own vases for the flowers."

It was quiet at the museum and Lily pulled her minivan right up front. She opened the side door and got one bouquet and Kirk's arrangement. "Daisy, can you grab the other bouquet?"

Daisy was standing by the fence looking into the museum garden. "Lily, look over there." Daisy pointed to a clump of dark green leaves.

Lily's eyes popped. "Monkshood. And it looks like some have been dug up."

Chapter 12

Maggie walked out of the museum and stopped next to Lily. "You're just in time to meet the evil stepdaughter." She continued on her way, laughing to herself.

Daisy asked Lily, "Evil stepdaughter? Who was she talking about?"

"I don't know but I've got goose bumps all over. This museum brings nothing but distressing feelings after what happened at the opening. It's all flashing back. Having Marion Barry dead in my arms—that dead weight was like a lifeless sack of potatoes. Let's get these flowers where they belong and get out of here."

Kirk Stevens was inside talking to a woman. "Lily, come meet my daughter. I've been telling her all about your arrangements. Do you have the one I requested? With monkshood?"

"Yes. Where do you want me to put it?" She showed him the basket filled with monkshood and white lilies.

"Very nice. What do you think Brandy?"

Brandy was busy studying her nails giving the impression that she was totally bored with the situation. She leaned against the wall with her legs crossed and her brown hair hanging down around her face. Her skirt was a bit too short for the occasion and her age Lily thought. *How old was Kirk when she was born?*

Brandy looked up. "Yeah. Whatever."

Lily felt she had to say something in this awkward situation. "I'm sure you are very upset about your mother. I'm terribly sorry."

Brandy glanced at Kirk. "She was my stepmother. Not exactly my favorite person."

Kirk's leg was nervously bouncing on the ball of his foot. He stroked Brandy's arm and laughed anxiously. "I'm sure she would appreciate it to know you flew all the way from California to come to the memorial gathering."

Brandy ignored that comment. "When can we get out of here?"

"Come on, honey. I'll show Lily where to put the flowers and then I'll take you home."

She shrugged. "I'll wait here."

Lily and Daisy followed Kirk. He kept looking back at Brandy until they entered another room. "This is where the memorial gathering will be. You can put the flowers here, just inside the door. Sorry to have to run, but, well—"

Lily interrupted, saving him from having to make up some excuse for Brandy's rude behavior. "We're all set."

Kirk hurried back to where Brandy was waiting. Daisy put her hand over her mouth. But once they were alone, the giggle escaped. "Wow. She's a prize. That must have been who Maggie was referring to."

Lily was trying not to laugh too hard. "Kirk has some history we don't know about. I'm guessing Brandy didn't like to share him with Elizabeth. For some reason she looks familiar to me." Lily got back to business. "I need to find Evelyn to get her vases for these bouquets." She walked to the back where the office was located.

"Listen Jared, you better come tonight. I don't care what you thought of my sister." Lily heard the sound of a phone slamming down.

Lily knocked on the door. Evelyn looked up and quickly put a smile on her face.

Lily asked, "I have the flowers. You said you have some antique vases?"

"Oh, yes." She looked around her office then got up. She walked into the hall. "They're in this closet."

As Evelyn reached in, Lily noticed a garden spade and dirty garden gloves pushed to the back. *Who would put dirty tools with valuable antiques?* She thought.

Evelyn quickly closed the door and showed the vases to Lily. "Will these work?"

"Yes. Perfect. Where do you want to put them?"

Evelyn walked to the front entrance. "One can go here on this table and the other will go in this other room where we will have the memorial gathering." She looked around. "Oh. You already put flowers here."

"Kirk ordered those. He wanted monkshood in Elizabeth's memory."

"Really? That sounds a little morbid after what happened to Marion." She pointed to another table. "You can put the other bouquet there. I have to get back to my office. Thank you so much Lily." Evelyn hurried off to the back of the museum.

Lily and Daisy fixed the flowers in the vases, fanning them out so they looked cheery. Lily looked around at the faces in the portraits staring at them. The museum felt cold and the quiet seeped into her bones. The quiet that makes you feel like something is lurking around every corner. "Let's get out of here. This place gives me the creeps."

Daisy mumbled, "Since when did you become such a nervous Nellie? Maybe tonight, with people here, it will feel warmer to you."

The rest of the afternoon flew by in a whirlwind of people coming and going in the shop. Lily didn't have time to think about all the events or to worry about the memorial for Marion and Elizabeth. Iris helped and Marigold was content to keep Sweet Pea company in the work room. The sound of the cash register and the phone ringing never seemed to stop. Jennifer and Katie took Rosie back to Ryan's house. She felt safe now with her ex in jail and with Rosie watching over Katie.

Lily was tired when she told Daisy it was closing time. "Let's clean up the shop and get out of here before anyone else walks in." Just as the words were out of her mouth, the door jingled and Nina Baldwin walked in. Lily saw who it was and frowned. *What could she want*? At least she didn't have her camera in front of her face snapping pictures already.

"Lily, I'm so glad I caught you before you closed. I have some photos I want to show you."

"I don't have time now. Maybe after the memorial at the museum? Are you going?"

Nina hesitated. "Someone has been following me. I finally got a shot of her and I was hoping you might be able to identify her."

Lily was surprised that Nina was asking her for help and she actually sounded subdued and a little worried. "Okay. Let me see."

Lily looked at the photo. It was through a car window and a little hard to see the details until Nina zoomed in. "Oh my goodness. Yes, I just met her today. That's Kirk Stevens' daughter." Lily looked up at Nina. "How long has she been following you?"

"I'm not sure but I've noticed her for at least the last couple of days."

"That's strange. When I met her, Kirk said she had just flown in from California. Are you coming tonight?"

"Do you think I should?"

"Definitely. And make sure you get lots of photos of her. Along with everyone else attending." Lily hesitated for a second. "Nina?" Lily put her hand on Nina's arm. "Don't take this the wrong way, but maybe you should try to be a little more casual. Try not to get right into people's faces."

Nina started to protest but stopped. "You're not the first person to tell me that. I'll work on it."

***

Iris picked up Lily just before seven. Marigold and Daisy were already in the car discussing how it wasn't the same exciting feeling they all had just a few nights ago on the way to the museum opening. *How could so much happen in such a short time?* Lily thought.

Surprisingly, the street outside the museum was lined with cars. There was probably a big curiosity factor for many of the people arriving. A double murder always brought that out in folks. Lily, Iris, Daisy and Marigold joined the line of people making their way into the museum. Somber cello music played in the background. It was a slow meander getting to the main room to give condolences to Evelyn and Kirk.

Of course, the folks going in all had theories about what happened since not much detail had been revealed yet. Lily did hear someone talk about poison and of course everyone had seen Lily's picture on the front of the paper with the stolen painting. She felt glances her way but she kept her head high and ignored it all.

The main room for the memorial gathering had a table set up with photos of Elizabeth and Marion. The flowers had been moved between those two displays. Iris leaned over to Lily. "Your flowers are about the only cheerful thing in this room." Until her eyes found

Kirk's daughter. She nudged Lily. "Look over there. Who is that? She looks like a street walker. "

Lily whispered to Iris, "That's Kirk's daughter. She's a real prize." Lily couldn't believe that she was dressed in a too short, too tight, red dress. About as inappropriate for this occasion as it could be. She was making some kind of statement as she clung to Kirk's arm.

Nina strolled over to Lily to say hi and showed Lily that she had her iPhone instead of the big camera she usually used for her job. "I took your advice. I won't look as obvious with this. I got here early and already have a boatload of photos."

The line was winding around the room so everyone could talk to Evelyn and Kirk. Evelyn pulled Lily aside when she reached them. "Have you seen Ruth yet?"

"I just got here. I haven't seen her."

Evelyn scanned the room. "Oh, she's just coming in. Please keep an eye on her for me."

Lily turned to see Ruth, dressed all in black from her hat and veil down to her pointy black shoes. It was certainly an outfit from another era but somehow it suited Ruth's nasty personality. She was alone and staring at Evelyn.

Kirk looked at ease except for his occasional nervous glances at Brandy who looked like this was the last place she wanted to be.

Evelyn clapped her hands and told the gathering that she was going to say a few words about her sister. "The museum will continue as it always has. Marion was generous and handed it over to me in her will. I won't be—"

Ruth screeched, "That wasn't in her will. She wanted it to go to the town of Misty Valley."

The room fell silent for three seconds, then buzzed with chatter. Lily noticed Nina warily documenting it all with her phone.

Evelyn tried to get control. "Yes, Marion did consider that option but after consulting with me, she didn't change her original will. I want everyone here to know that the Misty Valley Museum will continue as always and I'm appointing my son, Jared, to be the new director." She put her arm around Jared and smiled like a proud mother.

Kirk's face turned into an angry, dark sneer. He stormed from the room with Brandy click-clacking after him on her high heels.

Maggie appeared at Lily's side. "I told you. Evil stepdaughter. Fireworks. My mother doesn't have a clue what she's doing."

Lily scanned the room and couldn't see Ruth anywhere. She went out the way Kirk had gone and saw Nina ahead of her. Ruth was at the closet door taking the garden spade out. Lily grabbed Nina's arm and pulled her into an alcove so they wouldn't be seen but they could hear voices coming from the office.

Lily whispered in Nina's ear, "Go find Ryan Steele. I'm going to listen to what's going on in there."

Nina was wide eyed. "Are you sure?"

"Yes. Go. And don't lose your phone with those photos."

Lily tiptoed closer to the open office door. She sensed someone behind her but then everything went black.

Chapter 13

Lily opened her eyes to see her mother's face. Iris's mouth was moving but Lily couldn't hear any words. She focused on the smile lines around Iris' mouth as they smoothed out when she talked. Ryan crouched down next to her. Concern was written all over his face. His wonderful scent drifted to her nose. She noticed how extremely handsome he was; the dark shaggy hair and deep chocolate eyes that she was getting lost in. Slowly, the sounds around her started to register.

"Lily. Lily. What happened?" She looked from one face to another with no reply. She stared and tried to remember but she didn't even know where she was or why she was lying on a cold hard floor.

Tamara's voice penetrated the fog. "She must have a concussion. What was she doing back here anyway? Did she fall?"

Nina pushed her way next to Ryan. "We were following someone. All dressed in black. And Kirk Stevens and that woman in red. Lily told me to get you." Nina's voice trembled, obviously shaken up by the events.

Evelyn arrived all out of breath, took one look at Lily on the floor and fainted into Iris' arms. Iris lowered her to the floor. "She won't be any help."

Ryan checked the office and came out shaking his head. "No one is in there. Nina, did you hear or see anything else?"

"We saw the woman in black take a garden spade out of the closet. We hid in that alcove so we didn't see where she went but we could hear people in the office. Lily must have gone closer after I left."

Ryan picked Lily up and gently placed her on a small couch in the office. He stroked her cheek. She squeezed his hand and her mouth crinkled a little at the edge. Relief flooded his voice. "Now that I can see you're going to be alright, I ought to knock you out myself for being so careless." He looked around, searching for Iris or Daisy. "Keep an eye on her. Don't let her get up." He strode out of the room on a mission.

Tamara helped Evelyn into the office. She was still a little shaky but would be fine, especially since Iris broke her fall as she fainted. Tamara fluttered around taking control, making sure Lily was comfortable and finding a chair for Evelyn.

Evelyn looked around the office. "What happened?"

Ryan came back in with the garden spade. "Is this yours, Evelyn?"

She blanched. "Where did you get it?"

"It was outside the back door. Nina saw Ruth take it out of your closet in the hall." He didn't take his eyes from her face. She looked everywhere but at Ryan.

Maggie rushed into the office, saving Evelyn from answering Ryan's question. "Mom, are you okay? Jared said you fainted."

Evelyn got up from the chair. "I need to get back to the memorial before everyone has more to gossip about."

Maggie started to follow but Ryan held her arm. "Wait a minute. I have some questions for you."

Her face took on a blank expression.

"Did you leave the main room?"

"I'm here now."

"Okay. A smart aleck. Did you leave at any time before you came to find your mother?"

Maggie started to walk away, then turned and looked at him with disdain. "I don't have to answer your questions. Why don't you ask Kirk Stevens where he went? And while you're at it, what about that woman he's trying to pass off as his daughter? Have you seen how they act when they think no one is watching?" She smiled when she saw the shocked looks on their faces. "I guess you hadn't noticed that yet," she said as she left the office.

Tamara was the first to respond. "That girl needs a good kick in the butt. She is the rudest thing I've seen in a long time. What did she mean about Kirk and his daughter?"

Nina was scanning through her photos. "Look at this. I have it all here. I was here early and was taking photos of the paintings. Kirk and his daughter are in the background in the hall here. It's kind of blurry but it sure looks like she's all over him. More like a lover than a daughter."

Ryan took her phone. "Why would he pretend she was his daughter?"

Iris rolled her eyes. "Are you serious Ryan? He had a wife who was just murdered a few days ago. How would that look to show up at a memorial gathering with a hot younger girlfriend?"

Lily tried to sit up but couldn't quite manage. "Can someone get me some water?"

Nina rushed back with a cup of water. "Look what I found in the bathroom." She held up a brass sculpture of a tulip.

Ryan carefully took it from Nina and examined it. At the top, between two petals, he pulled out a couple strands of blonde hair. "This looks like Lily's hair. I'll get this checked for prints."

Lily finally managed to prop herself up on one arm. "Nina, check your other camera with the photos from the opening. See if she's in any of those."

Nina was excited. "I don't have it with me. Maybe that's why she's been following me."

Ryan watched Nina. "Why didn't you tell me about being followed?"

"I—ah—didn't think it meant anything."

Lily was sitting up. "I feel a lot better. Let's get back to the memorial and see what's going on there."

Daisy sat next to Lily. "I'll stay here with you." She looked at the others. "Lily's right. You should get back out there. Nina, keep taking photos." Everyone reluctantly left.

Lily grinned and said to Daisy, "Are you thinking what I'm thinking?"

Daisy stood up and looked around the office. "Where do you want me to start?"

"Try the desk drawers."

"What are we even looking for?"

"Maybe we'll be lucky and there will be a folder marked 'murder information'." Lily laughed.

Daisy quietly opened the top middle drawer. Nothing but pens, markers and other office supplies, all neatly arranged in separate slots. The right side of the desk had two shallow drawers and one deep drawer and the left side had a drawer for hanging folders. Daisy started to open the top right drawer but changed her mind and pulled open the left drawer. Most of the folders had typed labels and a few were hand written. All the folders were arranged alphabetically according to a type of flower. "Nothing labeled 'murder information'," she noted as she quickly shuffled through the folders. "But let's take a look inside this one." She had a devious grin as she showed Lily a folder labeled 'Aconitum'.

Lily was excited. "Bring it over here. Aconitum, common name—monkshood." Daisy sat next to Lily as they looked through the file. It was filled with pages of detailed drawings and pictures of every part of the plant. Beautiful blue monkshood to a less common yellow variety. The last page in the folder was labeled 'The Queen of Poison'.

Lily picked up her tote and dropped the whole folder in.

Daisy was shocked. "What are you doing?"

"We need to spend more time looking at this."

"Looking at what?" A voice startled them. They both looked up to see Jared standing in the doorway.

"What are you two doing in here? This is my mother's office."

Lily put her hand to her head and felt the goose egg bump with crusty hair stuck to it. "I guess you didn't hear. Someone knocked me over the head and I needed a place to rest for a few minutes."

Jared frowned. "You look fine to me. You need to leave."

Lily slowly stood up with Daisy's help. "Congratulations on your appointment as director of the museum, Jared. It's too bad your aunt isn't around to share in your achievement."

His face softened a little and he seemed to puff out his scrawny chest. "I've got big plans for the museum. I want to bring it into the twenty-first century and move away from all these boring dingy flower paintings she was so fond of."

"Oh?"

"I have some installation art ideas and a big photography exhibit. Not just flowers."

"Well, I hope you still continue the Art in Bloom tradition. It's something everyone in town looks forward to. You might not know that since you haven't been living here."

Lily picked up her tote and walk past Jared holding onto Daisy's arm. She tried to remain calm, hoping he didn't see the corner of the folder sticking out of the tote.

"Wait a minute." Jared's grating voice stopped them cold. "Did you drop this?" He held out a set of car keys.

Lily took them. "Not mine. These belong to someone who owns a Honda."

Jared mumbled under his breath. "Must be Brandy's. What was *she* doing in here?"

Daisy giggled. "I can think of something she and Kirk might have been doing."

Jared's eyes narrowed to slits. "Kirk and Brandy?" His face turned to disgust as her meaning dawned on him. "You've got to be kidding."

Lily put the keys in her pocket. "I'll give them to Kirk."

By the time Lily and Daisy got back to the main room most people were gone. Evelyn was flitting around saying thank yous and goodbyes. Kirk was lurking in the background without Brandy. He looked angry and was watching Evelyn.

Lily made her way to stand next to Kirk. "Where's your daughter? Did she leave already?"

Kirk plastered a friendly smile on his face. "Brandy? She wasn't feeling well so I took her home."

"That's too bad. I'm sure she wouldn't want to miss the big event." Lily took the keys out of her pocket. "Does Brandy drive a Honda?"

Kirk ran his fingers through his hair. "What?"

"Does Brandy drive a Honda? Did she lose her keys? I found these and someone said Brandy drives a Honda."

"Where did you find them?"

"In Elizabeth's office. Well, I guess it's Evelyn's office now. On the couch."

His eye started to twitch. "What were you doing in Elizabeth's office?"

"I guess I could ask you the same thing about Brandy? So, are these her keys?"

"You ask a lot of questions, Ms. Bloom. Yes, I think they are." He took the keys and walked over to Evelyn who was finally standing alone.

Kirk put his hand on her shoulder, forcing her to turn and look at him. "I can't believe you did that Evelyn. I thought we had an agreement."

"I only said I would consider your offer to be the new director but I decided Jared is a better fit. I'm sure you understand." She patted his arm in a conciliatory manner.

He jerked away from her. "Don't patronize me. Understand? Why would I understand? This isn't how it was all supposed to end," he hissed. "You'll regret double crossing me."

Kirk scanned the room and his steely glare targeted Lily. He pointed a smooth finger in her direction before shouting, "You'll be sorry too."

The room was spinning around Lily. Everything was moving in slow motion like she was moving through Jell-o. Then everything went black. For the second time that night.

Chapter 14

Once again, Lily was looking up at faces staring down at her. But at least she was on something soft with a warm tongue licking her cheek. She moved her hand to pat Rosie.

"Lily, can you hear me?" Lily registered the sensations of Iris gently stroking her arm while Rosie licked her face.

"What happened?" she asked as she tried to sit up.

"Oh no you don't. You got up too soon after that whacking. You have to stay right here until tomorrow. I've got Rosie on guard and I'm staying with you tonight."

Lily was relieved to let her body relax back into the soft cushions of her couch. Her eyes moved around the room—Iris, Daisy, Marigold, Nina, Ryan, Jennifer and Katie were all watching her.

Katie ran over, putting her head between Lily and Rosie. "Are you okay? Can I see your booboo?" she asked as only a five year old would.

Lily smiled and turned her head for Katie's inspection. Rosie immediately licked it clean of dried blood. "That's gross," Katie squealed, watching Rosie.

Jennifer gently took Katie's hand. "Time for bed. I said we'd wait till Lily woke up. You can visit again tomorrow."

Spontaneously, Katie hugged Lily and kissed her cheek. "I'm glad you're okay."

Lily watched them leave. "What happened? I can't remember anything except someone pointing at me."

"We'll talk about it tomorrow. You need to get some sleep." Iris covered her with a blanket and shooed everyone out the door.

Lily drifted into a restless sleep. She was trying to run away from someone but couldn't move. There was always someone hiding around every corner but never a face to see who it was. Finally, she opened her eyes to see the sun streaming in the window. That made all the ghosts in her head evaporate.

Iris helped her sit up and gave her a steaming hot cup of tea. "Let's start with this before you try to get up. You've got a bump on your head the size of an extra-large egg."

Lily sipped the tea. It felt hot and good, warming her from the inside out. "What happened?"

"Do you remember anything?"

Lily thought. "We were at the museum. I remember being in that office with Daisy. Something happened but I don't remember."

The back door opened and a deep cheery voice yelled a hello. The delicious aroma of muffins straight from the oven hit Lily's nose and she instinctively sucked in her gut, remembering her vow to cut out carbs. *Oh well*, she thought, *one more day before starting to work on the muffin top won't make a difference.*

Ryan walked in with Katie dancing by his side. "Jennifer made you some muffins if you feel up to eating anything."

"Smells scrumptious. You bet I'll eat one, maybe even two, before I go to work."

Iris and Ryan both frowned at her.

"What? I'm feeling good. I can't just sit around here all day, I'll go crazy."

Ryan looked at Iris. "I have to go to work. I'll let you deal with your stubborn daughter. Come on Katie. Jennifer is taking you to the playground today."

Iris grinned at Lily. "You can stop sucking in your gut now. You certainly weren't doing it to impress me."

"What? You could tell?"

"If Marigold was here, she would have been able to tell. Listen, honey, just be yourself. You're much more interesting with all your imperfections. Perfect is not remarkable."

"I was just trying to be perfect like you, Mom." Lily managed to keep a straight face for about three seconds, then they both howled with laughter. "Are you coming to the shop with me to make sure I don't overdo it?"

"Do I need to?" Iris asked with a your-mother-knows-best look.

"Nope. I promise to take it easy and Daisy will be there to help."

Lily savored every crumb of the muffins, even licking her fingers. "Ryan is gonna get fat if Jennifer stays with him. She's a great cook and she seems to like it too. I hope she always makes enough for me."

"Go take a shower. See how that goes and then decide about going to work."

The hot water pelting on her felt like it was washing all the fear away. She couldn't put her finger on what was making her feel fearful but there was something lurking in the background. She still couldn't remember what happened at the museum. Something happened and it had seeped into her dreams. Was someone out to get her? Work was the best remedy to clear her head.

Dressed in her usual uniform of jeans and a t-shirt, she was good to go. "I'm ready. Feeling like a new me."

Iris was skeptical but Lily was a big girl and she could learn the hard way if that was the way she wanted it. "Let's go. Do you want me to carry anything for you?"

"All I need is my tote. It should be here someplace but I can't find it. Not that important, maybe I left it at the shop."

Lily walked into chaos at her shop. Besides the phone ringing, customers lined up and Daisy furiously wrapping flowers, she inhaled the sweet scent of the flowers which always helped her feel better. This was her sanctuary whether it was hectic or quiet. Daisy looked up when the door jingled. "I've never been happier to see you, Lily. Get the phone, I'll take care of these customers." So much for a moment of reflection.

Lily jotted down the phone order and saw the list already waiting to get done. She hurried to the design area to get going on the list of orders. Jack, who was managing the local greenhouse, walked in the back door with buckets of flowers. "Where do you want these Lily? I've got snapdragons, alstroemeria, hybrid delphinium, dianthus and hosta leaves."

"Perfect timing. Put them wherever you can find room. I'll process them when I have time. Everything's in water already?"

"You bet. How are you feeling? I heard you got whacked last night."

Lily grinned. "I'm feeling pretty good, thanks for asking. News sure does travel fast in this town. I guess I shouldn't be surprised, you do have a direct link to Tamara and everyone knows how she likes to share news."

Jack nodded. "About as fast as a pat of butter melting on a hot griddle. Let me know if you need anything else."

"With the look of these orders, I'll need another delivery later in the week."

Lily finished up a couple of arrangements and put them in the cooler along with the ones Daisy had already made.

The rest of the day flew by without much peace and quiet. Lily and Daisy worked well together, anticipating what needed to get done or knowing when another pair of hands was needed to hold something. Lily knew she was lucky to have Daisy around and didn't know what she would do if Daisy decided on a different career. Lily was even thinking of expanding the flower shop and adding specialty chocolates so Daisy could have her own space. She didn't have the money yet for an expansion, but if business kept going at this pace it wouldn't be long.

Daisy flopped into the chair, picking up Sweet Pea and stroking her soft fur. "This was one long and busy day. I'm glad you weren't completely incapacitated or I would have had to have Mom help." They both rolled their eyes. Iris was great, but they both preferred not to work with her.

"Don't worry. I never plan to put you through that."

The door that had actually been quiet for the past half hour jingled and Daisy groaned. Lily peeked out front. "It's just Ryan."

"What do you mean, 'just Ryan'?" she teased. "Maybe it's time for me to head home. Can you finish up?"

Lily looked at the clock, shocked to see it was almost five. "Yeah, I'm fine. I'll make a few deliveries and then close up." She hugged Daisy. "Thanks. I couldn't do this without you."

"I know." Daisy was twinkling from the compliment, said hi to Ryan and left the shop.

Lily looked over to see Ryan casually leaning in the doorway to the design room, arms crossed and trying not to smile. She could see the edges of his mouth twitch just enough for her to know he was on the edge of a big toothy grin but was going to say something serious instead. She waited.

"Why did you go down the hall last night? Who were you following?"

Lily scrunched her face in deep concentration. "I don't remember."

"Come on Lily. This isn't a game. What were you and Nina doing?"

"Ryan. I really don't remember anything from last night except being in the office and someone pointing at me."

His face got serious. "I thought you were just trying to avoid answering my question."

"I wish that was the case. I tried to remember. I had bad dreams all last night—someone chasing me, but I could never see a face."

Ryan picked up Sweet Pea and sat in the chair, letting the cat get comfortable in his lap. "Something will trigger the memory. Are you almost done?"

"I have to make a few more deliveries, then close up. Why?"

"Nina is stopping at my house later to show me the photos on her two cameras. Come on over, maybe that will trigger something."

"Okay. Will there be food?"

"Probably. Jennifer loves to cook. I'll miss that when she finds her own apartment."

"You're a rotten brother. You'll miss her cooking but not her?"

He laughed. "Of course I'll miss Jennifer and Katie and the kitten I got as a surprise for Katie."

"Really? She'll be thrilled."

He stood up. "See you later?"

"I'll come for the food and your sister's company," she teased.

Ryan walked over to Lily. "I'll give you something else to miss." He put his arms gently around her waist and pulled her close. She could feel his heart beating through his shirt. The rhythm of the beat matched hers. She could get lost in his arms. "This is part one. If you're nice to me, you might get part two." He sighed and let her go.

Lily loaded the flowers into her van and got everything delivered in record time. She wanted part two from Ryan Steele.

Back at the shop she had to feed Sweet Pea, check the cooler and lock up. Her mind was already back in Ryan's arms when she walked in the back door of the shop.

"It's about time you got back here. I almost gave up."

Lily's blood ran cold at the sound of that voice. The voice was the trigger unlocking her memories of the night before.

Chapter 15

"Jared. What can I do for you?"

He held up her quilted tote. "You forgot this at the museum. I thought you might need it and the file you stole from my mother's desk. Interesting choice you made with that file."

Time seemed to stop as Lily watched Jared's mouth move. She thought it was odd and funny at the same time how she noticed everything in such vivid detail. His wrinkled khaki pants, worn at the bottom because he never bothered to get them hemmed to the proper length. His belt fastened in the third hole. The light blue oxford shirt buttoned right to the top. *Who buttons the top button?* His straight sandy blond hair hanging over his eyebrows between his eyes and his glasses. *That must be weird to see your own hair in front of everything.* His glasses with a fingerprint smudge on the left lens. The spotty stubble on his face. *He couldn't grow a beard if he tried, it would just be a patchy mess.* Back to his mouth that hadn't stopped moving while these thoughts ran through her head.

"I brought you something."

Lily's ears really perked up. "What did you bring?"

"Some cookies I made. Would you like to try one?"

Alarm bells blared in her head. *Eat something he brought? Not over my dead body. Well, that's not the best choice of words since dead is probably his intention.* "Not right now. They do look delicious. Can I save it for later?"

"Nice try. Eat it now."

Lily took a cookie. She needed to get him talking again and she needed to pay attention to the words. *Stroke him, flatter him, boost his ego, anything to kill—oops, another bad choice of words—the time.* "Tell me more about your plans for the museum. Have you thought about working with local artists?"

"What local artists? There's just a bunch of hacks in this red neck town."

"I think you'd be surprised. There's actually a lot of talent."

He pushed the hair out of his eyes. "I'll ask the questions. How did you figure out about Kirk and Brandy?"

Lily forced herself to look relaxed on the outside. "Maggie hinted at it."

"That traitor. I knew I couldn't trust her. I was hoping to get her locked up when I ditched the painting behind the museum for her to find. She always needs money for that drug habit and I was sick of supporting it."

Lily risked asking a question. "What about the stolen antiques that ended up at Uncommon Antiques?"

"Brilliant wasn't it? Made it look like Maggie again. She must have a guardian angel or something since she's always walking into trouble but hasn't gotten caught yet. And it certainly embarrassed Kirk."

Lily watched Sweet Pea getting ready to jump into Jared's lap. She wasn't sure how he would respond to that. Sweet Pea took the leap and curled up. Jared stroked her soft fur. "Nice cat. I do like cats. They're independent and sneaky," he said with a glint in his eye.

"How did you get Kirk to keep making Ruth look like the murderer?"

He smiled an evil smile. "Another brilliant move. Blackmail to keep his fake daughter a secret and I knew he wanted to be director. I planted those ideas and told him if he spread the information, I would put in a good word with my mother for him. I didn't plan on you going back to the museum after Marion died, but that took care of itself. Never hurts to have a couple of suspects—one for each dead body."

Lily was desperate to keep him rambling. "I see your cleverness. You thought of everything."

He relaxed back in the chair while Sweet Pea purred away. *Traitor,* Lily thought, looking at her cat.

"You know what the best part is?"

"It sounds like you can't wait to tell me."

He leaned toward Lily. "You stole the file with all the information about the monkshood and how it's poisonous." He sat back satisfied with that nugget.

Lily looked confused.

Sitting forward again, he glared at her. "Are you stupid? Do I have to spell everything out for you? Your fingerprints are all over it. It's here in your tote. Now, once you eat that cookie and you're dead in your shop, people will just think you died from that concussion on your head. And the file is the evidence pointing to you as the murderer. I was disappointed that the whack didn't kill you last night but it's actually working out better this way. Everyone will say, 'That Lily Bloom, she got just what she deserves.'"

Lily was getting more and more worried as he slipped farther into his warped delusional world. He actually seemed to think that everyone else would only see his conclusions and not any other more rational possibility. This did not bode well for her.

Sweet Pea jumped off his lap and stood by the back door. Lily looked at her and then at Jared. "She needs to go out."

"I'll let her out. No point in having her be traumatized watching you die. We're about to the end of this conversation."

Jared turned the doorknob. As the door opened a fraction, a white blur charged in knocking the unsuspecting Jared Nash to the floor. Rosie stood on his chest, baring her teeth and snarling right in his face.

He tried to protect himself but Rosie grabbed his arm, clamping down until he stopped struggling.

Lily was stunned for about two seconds before she grabbed her phone and dialed 911.

Police cars arrived in what seemed like seconds. Ryan handcuffed Jared and turned him over to his deputy.

Ryan took a long look at Lily, then wrapped his arms around her, asking if she was okay.

"Perfect now," she whispered.

He added before releasing her, "We have to stop meeting like this."

Lily never felt better as she let Rosie jump up and give a doggie kiss.

Iris rushed in with Daisy. "We leave you out of our sight for two shakes of a lamb's tail and you almost get yourself killed?"

Lily sank into the chair, her legs suddenly going all wobbly. "How did Rosie know?"

Iris patted Rosie. "I let her out when I got to your house to check how you were doing. She didn't even stop to pee. She just took off. I wasn't sure where she was going but I had a pretty good idea that she knew you needed help. How did she get into the shop?"

"Sweet Pea went to the door. I think she sensed that Rosie was waiting to come in. Jared opened the door to let Sweet Pea out and Lily crashed in like a bull."

Tears were streaming down Lily's cheeks from all the stress she just went through and the relief that it was over. Rosie's head was happily resting on Lily's lap. "This dog doesn't even know how special she is. I wish I could clone her."

Ryan asked Lily if she felt up to giving a statement.

"Yes. I think I need to get this out of my head now so I can move on to something more pleasant. And don't forget to take that cookie as evidence. I'm pretty sure he was planning to poison me the same way he poisoned his aunt."

Ryan pulled up a chair. "We can do it here if that's easier than going to the station."

Lily looked around at her beautiful shop. "No. I've been here long enough for one day. Let's go. Can Rosie stay with me?"

Ryan hesitated, then saw the urgency in Lily's eyes. "Sure. We can make an exception this time. Besides, I don't think she'll let you out of her sight for a while."

Ryan took Lily and Rosie to the station to get that wrapped up.

"I bet you're starving. Jennifer said she would save some food for us. What do you think?"

Lily yawned. "Some food and a good night's sleep."

Katie was still up, waiting to see Lily and Rosie when they finally made it home. "Look what Uncle Ryan gave me," she sang out when they walked in as she held up a tiny black kitten.

Rosie sniffed the kitten all over, then licked his face. The kitten batted his paws at Rosie's face. Lily crouched down. "He's adorable. Did you name him yet?"

Katie grinned from ear to ear. "His name is Posie. I think his bestest friend will be Rosie so they'll be Rosie and Posie."

Lily laughed. "That's about the bestest thing I've heard all day. You certainly are a lucky girl to have such a nice uncle."

Katie ran over and hugged Ryan. "Thank you. Thank you. Thank you. I love Posie." Katie looked at her mom. "Can Posie sleep with me tonight?"

"I don't see why not. And speaking of sleep, it is that time. Say good night to everyone."

Katie cuddled Posie in her arms as she sang out, "Good night."

Uncle Ryan answered, "Don't let the bedbugs bite."

Chapter 16

Lily relaxed completely with the sun warming her face. She drifted in and out of the conversations around her. The sound of kids playing and splashing in the lake was soothing.

"Lily, Lily. Look what I found." Katie ran over holding a smooth gray rock.

"Very pretty. Add it to this pile. Are you going to bring all of them home?"

Katie looked at Jennifer. "Can I Mommy?"

Jennifer smiled. "You can bring as many rocks as you can carry."

Lily jumped when she felt cold drops of water splashing on her stomach. Her eyes popped open to see Ryan blocking the sun. "What are you doing?"

"Get up. Come in the water with me." He held his hand out to help her up. "You've been sitting here long enough. You need some exercise to work off all that food."

Lily's eyes blazed. "What did you say? Come a little closer. I'm not sure I heard you right."

Ryan stepped closer. Lily hooked her foot around the back of his knee and watched him fall into the sand on his butt.

Ryan pushed himself up and grabbed Lily's arm. "You're in trouble now." Ryan picked her up and swung her over his shoulder. She screamed all the way to the water's edge.

"You wouldn't dare, Ryan Steele."

He kept going and dunked her in the lake. When she came up for air, he asked, "Wouldn't dare what?"

Lily knocked him over and held him under water until he freed himself. He grabbed her around her waist. "Now I've got you where I want you."

She stopped struggling and rested her face against his wet chest. "When are you going to tell me the rest of the story about Jared?"

"If you beat me swimming out to the raft, I'll tell you."

Lily took off and got a good head start. She touched the raft one hand length before Ryan and gloated with a big smile. "Let's sit on the raft in the sun and you can tell me the story now."

"You cheated. I never said get ready, set, go."

She climbed onto the raft. "Quit whining and tell me the details. That's the only way I'll be able to get it all out of my head and concentrate on something else." She winked. "Like you, if you're nice to me."

"You drive a hard bargain, Lily Bloom. Okay. Here's what happened before we found you at the shop. Nina came to my house with her cameras and we studied all the shots. She found photos of Brandy at the opening even though Kirk had said she just came from California for the memorial. That ended up not to be very important, just embarrassing for Kirk. I heard he may be closing his business and moving out of town."

"Was she following Nina?"

"Yeah, Brandy was afraid Nina might put two and two together about her and was trying to intimidate her."

"What about the stolen antiques?"

"That was Jared. We found a girl he paid to bring them to Kirk. When Kirk told you a girl brought them in, you jumped to the conclusion it was Maggie. I think that was Jared's intention."

"What about Ruth? She acted so guilty and her bag with the gloves with blood on them."

"The blood was hers. She must have cut herself. Ruth didn't know who she could trust so she lashed out at everyone trying to help her."

Lily rolled onto her stomach. Ryan tickled her foot. She kicked at him. "Hey. Finish the story."

"The important photo was of Kirk pointing. You thought he was pointing at you but in the photo we saw Jared standing a little behind you and realized that Kirk was pointing at Jared."

Lily shivered.

"Are you cold?"

"Not cold. Thinking about Jared gives me goose bumps."

"When Iris came in to my house and said Rosie had taken off, we all knew you were in trouble. I headed straight to your shop."

Lily's eyes were half closed. She murmured, "Before I dialed 911?"

"Even before. The rest is all Rosie's story. You know that part."

Thank you was all she could manage to say before she fell asleep in the warm afternoon sun.

ABOUT THE AUTHOR

Lyndsey Cole lives in New England in a small rural town with her husband, dogs, cats and chickens. She has plenty of space to grow lots of beautiful perennials. Sitting in the garden with the scent of lilac, peonies, lily of the valley or whatever is in bloom, stimulates her imagination about mysteries and romance.

ONE LAST THING . . .

If you enjoyed this installment of Lily Bloom Cozy Mystery Series, be sure to join my FREE COZY MYSTERY BOOK CLUB! Be in the know for new releases, promotions, sales, and the possibility to receive advanced reader copies. Join the club here—
http://LyndseyColeBooks.com

OTHER BOOKS BY LYNDSEY COLE

Begonia Means Beware

Stay tuned for the next book in the Lily Bloom Cozy Mystery Series.

Coming Summer 2014!!

If you enjoyed *Queen of Poison*, the second of the Lily Bloom Cozy Mystery Series, check out *Deadly Surprise*, the second of The Early Bird Café Series—written by my daughter!

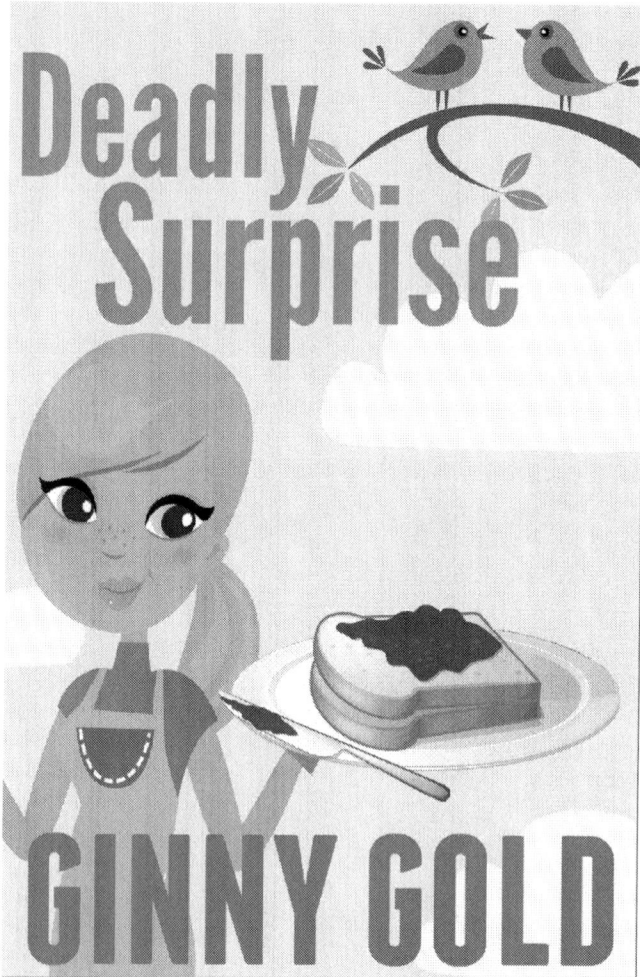

Kori is over the moon excited to be going on a date with none other than Lieutenant Zach Gulch, childhood crush and stunner to look at. But that thrill is quickly stifled the next day when Zach reveals that family DNA showed up at a crime scene in nearby Scoter Circle.

They both know the DNA isn't Kori's but it belongs to a close male relative. With her father long dead and her cousin Tyler living across the country, that only leaves Jay as a suspect. And it turns out his gun was also in the right place at the wrong time to pin everything on him.

Now, Kori and Jay have a list of online dating profiles that become the top suspects, starting with the deceased's violent ex-husband. Will they be able to find the real killer before Jay is behind bars with a guilty conviction for a murder he barely knows anything about? And why did the murderer try to frame him—he hadn't been in touch with Heidi for years.

As the questions pile up, they hope the body count stays at one.

CHAPTER 1

Kori was nervous beyond belief. She couldn't believe she'd said yes. She was going on a date with Zach Gulch. After nearly twenty years of pretending she didn't have feelings for him, here she was getting all dolled up and was as jumpy as a teenager.

"Where is he taking you?" Nora asked, seated on Kori's bed. Kori knew she wouldn't be able to make all the important decisions about what to wear and how to do her hair so she'd asked her best friend to come over.

"Jackson's," Kori said, turning around to gauge Nora's reaction. Jackson's was located on the north side of Thrush Lake, looking south toward Hermit Cove. The outside seating was perfectly located so they would be able to look back at their hometown while they enjoyed the fanciest meal in the state.

"I can't believe he could get a table so fast!" Nora reacted exactly how Kori knew she would—shouting in excitement and leaping off the bed. Kori blushed and turned back to the mirror to work on her makeup.

"Let me do that," Nora said, coming up beside her and taking the mascara from her hand. "You're shaking and you're just going to smudge it."

It was true. Kori gladly let Nora take over. They were celebrating the two month anniversary of Kori clearing her name and solving the first murder case in Hermit Cove in decades and she wanted to look her best.

"Have you decided what you're going to wear?" Kori was still wrapped in a towel, a second one on her head drying her hair.

"No. That's why you're here," Kori joked, but she was dead serious.

"Well, let's think about this. It's late May so it could still be cold at night. What time is your reservation?"

"Seven. He's picking me up in half an hour," Kori said as calmly as she could while her heart beat against her ribs at the thought of how soon she'd be with Zach.

"You'll want something that will keep you warm enough. I'm almost done with your makeup and then we're going to raid your closet."

Nora put the finishing touches on Kori's face and then stepped back to admire her work. "Look in the mirror," Nora instructed her. "What do you think?"

"You do amazing work." Kori couldn't take her eyes off herself. She wasn't usually vain, but she looked great. Her eyes popped and the color on her cheeks wasn't overdone.

"Now, to the closet!" Nora wasted no time with dawdling. She took off as if she were headed for the Batcave.

Inside Kori's closet they start rifling through the few dresses Kori had acquired over the years. She had the dress she'd worn to a friend's wedding in New York years ago, but it was strapless and wouldn't work in this weather. There was the dress she'd bought for almost nothing at a consignment shop just before a vacation to the beach. But it wasn't formal enough for this evening.

"This is it," Nora said, pulling a fitted maroon dress from its hanger. Kori'd had it altered years ago and had never had a reason to wear it. Until now. A friend, who was a bit heftier than Kori's size six, had given it to her. After paying pennies to have it adjusted, it fit her perfectly.

"But it has no sleeves. And it doesn't come past my knees. I'll be cold," Kori protested.

"You have a white sweater?" Nora asked, checking what else was in the closet. She pulled a cashmere cardigan off a hanger. "Here, put this on too."

Kori took the towel off of her head and let her wet hair fall down her back. She knew Nora wouldn't let her get away with her usual ponytail tonight. She slipped the dress over her head and let it slide down her body and at the same time she let the towel fall away.

"Zip?" Kori asked and turned around so Nora could zip the back.

"Perfect," Nora said, admiring Kori. "Sit on the bed. I'll do your hair."

Kori paused in front of the mirror and took in her new look. Her chest had never been her proudest feature, but the tightness of the dress accentuated it just enough to make her take a second glance. And the underwire bra did miracles. She was glad she'd decided to take the time to shave her legs.

Finally, Kori did as instructed and sat on her bed. She wondered where Nora got her fashion sense since farming required her to usually dress in baggy overalls and boots but she loved that her best friend complemented her own complete lack of any desire to be fashionable.

Nora plugged in the hair dryer and got to work. They were running out of time. She combed while she dried and ended up with perfectly straight, flowing blonde hair. A side part let some hair fall in front of Kori's face, making her even more enticing.

As soon as the hair dryer was turned off, the doorbell rang and Kori gave Nora a look of fear. "Don't worry. This is *Zach*," Nora reminded her. "You've known him your whole life."

Kori nodded. "Right. I'll get the door. Let yourself out after we leave."

"Have such a great time." Nora hugged Kori and started cleaning up the makeup and hair accessories. "Remember, let him treat you like the princess you are."

Kori slipped on her sandals—she could only hope that they matched her dress since they hadn't had time to work through that piece of her outfit—and headed quickly downstairs through The Early Bird Café and opened the front door. In front of her was heart stopping Zach Gulch, childhood crush she'd always thought was out of her league.

"Wow," he said, eyes growing wide with lust. She watched his smile spread and she returned it with one of her own. "Not only am I finally taking Kori Cooke out to dinner, but she looks . . . beautiful."

Kori smiled and looked at her feet quickly. "You look great, too," she said shyly, looking back up into Zach's eyes. Those eyes. She couldn't get enough of them. They were swimming pool blue and made her think of summer.

"Ready to go?" he asked and offered his arm.

Kori gladly accepted and walked to his car.

***

Once Zach and Kori were seated at their table at Jackson's—right on the water—Kori's nerves picked up again. She'd relaxed in the car with the radio to distract her but now that it was just the two of them, her words seemed to have sunk to the bottom of the lake.

"Business picking up for the summer?" Zach asked, seemingly unaware of her inability to make conversation.

"It is. And it doesn't hurt that The Early Bird is the only café in town again." She could have kicked herself under the table at bringing up her rival's murder.

Zach just chuckled. "I'm sure it doesn't. Something to drink?" he asked, picking up the drink menu and looking it over. "A bottle of wine?"

"That'd be great."

"Red or white?"

"Red."

"Are you cold?" he asked, concern in his voice.

Kori shook her head. She was actually sweating from the adrenaline coursing through her veins but shivering at the same time from nervousness. She couldn't figure out why she couldn't reel in her nerves. She'd known Zach her whole life, what was wrong with her tonight?

The waiter came to their table and Zach ordered a bottle of red wine and a fried calamari appetizer. Kori wondered, *How is he so calm?*

"How's work going for you?" she finally asked when the waiter had walked away. *Really? Work?* She chided herself for being so lame.

Zach didn't seem to care. "Quiet since Tessa's murder. Now it's back to DUIs and speeding tickets."

"That's a good thing, right?" Kori asked.

"Yes. We don't need another murder in Hermit Cove."

They were interrupted again with the wine arriving. Zach tasted it and approved the bottle before both of their glasses were filled.

Zach held up his glass and Kori mirrored him. "To a quiet future," he said and their glasses clinked together gently. She quickly wondered if he meant the future in general or theirs specifically. That thought made her smile.

The first sip immediately calmed Kori and she started to enjoy herself more, letting herself admire Zach for the person he was—down to earth, kind and always ready to give a hand to someone in need.

"Hey, have you hired another detective since Gunn was arrested?"

"Yup. Just yesterday. Detective Lani Silver."

"A girl?" Kori wasn't sure why she was surprised.

Zach nodded in confirmation and then changed the subject. "Tell me about your life in New York City." Kori easily slipped into stories from the years she lived away from Hermit Cove and started to thoroughly enjoy the evening.

She told stories and watched his body respond to her words. His blue eyes sparkled when he laughed; his broad shoulders relaxed more with each story; his short hair reflected the setting sun, giving it a tinge of red. Her heart was racing faster and faster as she looked at his muscular body.

She finally understood why she'd been so nervous—she desperately wanted this relationship to work.

***

Zach pulled up to the Early Bird Café just after ten that night. Kori sat in the passenger seat longer than she'd intended hoping the night wouldn't end.

"Tonight was, well—" Kori looked at Zach, temporarily speechless. She tried again. "I had an awesome time tonight," she told him, her nerves totally gone after the hours they'd spent together chatting about everything.

"Me too." Zach returned her gaze and put his arm around Kori.

"Thanks for taking me out. I can't even think of the last time I went out to dinner."

"It was my pleasure. We could do it again if you wanted."

Kori smiled and leaned slightly toward Zach. He met her halfway and they kissed for the first time after years of avoiding their true feelings. She had imagined this kiss many times but the real thing was so much better.

"Good night, Zach," Kori said, slightly speechless.

"Good night, Kori."

Kori let herself out of the car and into her café. She couldn't remember walking upstairs but somehow she made it to her living room. She sat on the couch, turned the TV on and relived the last several hours. Her eyes were unseeing but the sound of whatever show was on was a welcome sound. Eventually she headed to the bathroom to wash her face free of the makeup Nora had so expertly applied and brush her teeth before going to bed.

At four the next morning her alarm rang and Kori slowly opened her eyes. She was still on a high from her date and knew that today would be a good day.

It was Sunday, often the busiest day for her. She pulled on a pair of jeans and a black t-shirt and headed downstairs to get everything ready.

She started with the coffee. She didn't offer anything fancy, just a variety of roasts including coffee from Kona, Hawaii—a personal favorite—Tanzania, Ethiopia and Guatemala. She added additional varieties sometimes, depending on what was available in bulk and for what price. She had large pots that customers could order on the go, or if they were staying for a meal she ground fresh beans and served them in a French press.

Today she would make Kona and Ethiopian in the large pots and she got them going right away.

Then she headed to the walk-in freezer and fridge. Yesterday before she'd left for the day she'd made squash and sage biscuit dough. She took that out and set it on the counter. Everything else had been eaten and she'd have to make everything from scratch this morning.

Belgian waffles were easy, so those immediately went down as a menu option. She would make whipped cream that she would pair with strawberries. Or maple syrup.

She also had plenty of veggies from Nora's Red Clover Farm including kale and spinach, which were great additions to smoothies. Mixed with frozen fruit, yogurt and a little juice, green smoothies were a great Sunday morning breakfast side.

With granola, she'd add yogurt and fruit. And finally, she needed egg options. Feeling overly ambitious after last night, she considered popovers and huevos rancheros.

All of this went on the three chalkboard menus painted directly on the walls and then she set to work getting everything ready.

Fruits were placed next to the blender with yogurt, milk and juice nearby. Containers of granola, more yogurt and fruit were placed next to tall stemmed glasses that she'd serve them in. Waffle batter was whipped up and she placed that next to the waffle press, followed by whipped cream, strawberries and syrup. She made popover batter and took out her four popover pans. They had to bake for longer than anything else so she even stuck one pan in the preheated oven to get them started before she opened. And finally, she got gravy started and placed the first tray of biscuits in the oven as well.

Kori was feeling proud of her early morning energy when she glanced at the clock. It was already ten to six and she hadn't unlocked the door or flipped the sign to open! She'd never been so engrossed in her work that she'd forgotten to open on time at five thirty but there was a first for everything.

She quickly walked to the front of the café and opened the door. She was happy to see Jenna and Kyle Rhodes patiently waiting outside for her to open.

"Sorry for the delay," Kori told them as she held the door for them to enter.

"No worries. We didn't want to rush you so we walked up and down Main Street and enjoyed the quiet," Jenna told her. Then asked with a smile, "Late night last night?" Jenna winked and Kori blushed.

"No later than usual. I got so caught up in my cooking and getting everything ready that I didn't notice the time. Can I get you some coffee to start?"

Jenna and Kyle sat across from each other in a booth by the front windows with a view of Main Street.

"Black coffee for me. Kona," Jenna said, glancing at the menu to see what was available. Kyle held up two fingers to indicate he'd take the same.

Kori headed back to the kitchen and ground some beans, put them in a French press and poured hot water over them. She brought that to their table with two mugs.

"What are you putting in your smoothies?" Jenna asked when Kori set everything down on their table.

"There are plenty of options for you to choose from. I have kale or spinach for the greens, apple juice, orange juice or coconut water for the liquid, and bananas, strawberries, blueberries, blackberries, pineapple and mango for the fruits. And a yogurt base. Do you think you want one?"

"Not sure yet. Give us a couple more minutes," Jenna requested, looking at her husband and seeing that he was nowhere near knowing what he wanted.

"Sure." Kori turned and headed to the oven to check on the popovers and biscuits. Both were ready so she took them out and got seconds of both ready to be popped into the oven once more customers arrived.

The door opened just then and Kori looked up to see who had entered. A group of three adults came inside, looking slightly lost—tourists, she assumed—and Betsy Scoop was with Vera Joy, the owner of Furry Friends, the animal shelter across the street from The Early Bird. Kori didn't wait for anyone to order popovers or biscuits and gravy; she put the second trays of each in the oven and headed back out to make the rounds.

Kori started an easy conversation with Betsy and Vera, two people she had known for a long time. "Good morning. How's the move for Scoop's Scoops going?" she asked Betsy who looked up and smiled.

"All moved in! Can you believe how late I'm opening? I can't believe it took almost two months since the whole disaster with Tessa for things to get finalized," Betsy told her, visibly more relaxed now that she'd be able to open her business

Two months ago, Hermit Cove had seen its first murder in years—something that everyone was worried would put a damper on the summer tourist season. Tessa Doyle, the owner of a second café, had been murdered and Kori had been the prime suspect given their unfriendly past as students and near colleagues in New York City. Instead of landing in jail, Kori had cracked the case and Betsy had been able to move her ice cream shop, Scoop's Scoops, into the larger area that had been occupied briefly by the café.

"That's great to hear. Are you opening today?"

"I am. I can't wait. I have two high school sophomores working for me and I'm so excited to be able to expand so much this year."

"Congratulations!" Kori said with genuine excitement. She was happy for her friend and also for Hermit Cove's growing popularity. "And how are the cats and dogs?" she asked, turning to Vera.

"I was hoping you'd ask. I just got the perfect dog for you—she's four, so a little older, but friends with everyone. It was an owner surrender. I know you keep saying you're not ready, but I'm telling you, this dog is for you."

Kori looked down at her feet. She wanted to adopt a dog so badly but had been putting it off because she worked such long days and didn't want to leave a pet home alone all day. She didn't think that was fair to the animal.

"And the best part is that she used to go to a retirement home as a casual therapy dog, so you know she'd be fine in the café with customers." Vera's face was full of hope.

"I'll think about it," Kori finally managed. And she would. "What can I get you started with?"

The rest of the morning proved as busy as it started with the wait getting as long as twenty minutes. Kori knew she was almost in Betsy's position of needing to hire help—at least for the summer—and possibly even expand. The café only seated twenty people, so she could usually keep up with the rush. But if she didn't have to, why was she still pushing herself?

Midway to lunch, Kori's heart started fluttering when she saw Zach Gulch walk in with who she assumed was his new detective, Lani Silver. She tried to study her from afar and was disappointed to see that she was gorgeous: at least six feet tall, soft features that were easy to look at and a smile that got men turning their heads away from their breakfasts. *Could Zach possibly be attracted to her? Had he hired her because she would be nice to look at every day?*

They took a seat at the counter in front of the window where she worked and Kori was suddenly speechless.

"Morning Kori. I thought I'd give Detective Silver the grand tour of Hermit Cove this morning and we're finishing up here."

Kori managed to croak out a reply, "You're already finished? It's not even noon yet. There's got to be more to see in Hermit Cove."

"Well, we stopped by Red Clover Farm, Furry Friends, the market, the rec center, the auto body, post office and school—even though they were closed for Sunday—and now we're here." Zach's smile this morning had the same reaction in Kori's knees as it'd had last night. Only this time she was standing so had to look away before they buckled right beneath her. *But was the smile only for her or was part of it reserved for the amount of time he was going to be spending with Detective Silver?*

"Welcome to Hermit Cove," Kori managed to sputter to her new competition for Zach's heart. She tried to keep her voice calm and friendly but wasn't sure she'd managed completely. "Can I get you both something? On the house. As a welcome-to-Hermit-Cove gift," she added quickly, not wanting Lani to think that she always treated Zach that way. Or maybe she should let her think that; make sure she knew he was off limits. But was he? Had she really staked enough claim after just one date?

"I'll take one of the smoothies," Zach said. "Thanks."

There was that smile again that left Kori's knees weak and her heart skipping a couple of beats.

"Thanks Kori. Just a coffee. Black," Lani ordered.

Kori was relieved and disappointed that she couldn't stay to chat with Lani, but especially with Zach. Last night had been such an eye opener for her that she wanted it to continue right away but she also wanted to be sure that she was going down a path she was ready for. She wasn't quite sure how to balance those two emotions—and keep Lani at bay if there was any interest there.

At one, Kori finally sat down. She didn't even have the energy to close and lock the door first but everyone in town knew she was closed. It was only tourists she'd have the chance of having to turn away.

Suddenly the door opened. She looked up from the discarded newspaper she was reading, ready to apologize to whoever had entered, and saw her brother's worried face. "What is it?" she asked.

"It's Heidi. She's dead."

To keep reading, <u>purchase *Deadly Surprise* today!</u>

34101239R00079

Made in the USA
Lexington, KY
25 July 2014